PENGUIN BOOKS

DUXTON HILL: A ROMANTIC COMEDY

Mark Powell was born in Sevenoaks, Kent, in 1963 and now lives in Singapore. He's an award-wining novelist, playwright and screenwriter. Known as an explosive storyteller, Mark delivers brutally realistic fiction with strong, clever and fearless characters. He credits his adventurous and fun childhood for his creative talents. He writes in several genres including thriller, action and adventure, romantic comedy and mystery, for adults and young adults.

His published works include: *Quantum Breach* (Marshall Cavendish, 2009), *Deep Six* (Marshall Cavendish, 2010), *The Somali Sanction* (Amazon, 2012), *The Adventures of Danny Dare* (Amazon, 2013), *16 Swipes: No Breakfast* (Marshall Cavendish, 2019), *16 Swipes, The Other Perspective* (Penguin Random House SEA, 2021), *Bad Juice* (Amazon, 2022) and now his latest novel, *Duxton Hill*. In the works are: *The Silver Spoon Club* and *Escape*.

Also by Mark Powell

16 Swipes, The Other Perspective: 16 Women's Adventures Through Tinder, 2021, Penguin Random House SEA

Duxton Hill:
A Romantic Comedy

Mark Powell

PENGUIN BOOKS

An imprint of Penguin Random House

PENGUIN BOOKS

USA | Canada | UK | Ireland | Australia
New Zealand | India | South Africa | China | Southeast Asia

Penguin Books is part of the Penguin Random House group of companies
whose addresses can be found at global.penguinrandomhouse.com

Published by Penguin Random House SEA Pte Ltd
9, Changi South Street 3, Level 08-01,
Singapore 486361

Penguin
Random House
SEA

First published in Penguin Books by Penguin Random House SEA 2022

10 9 8 7 6 5 4 3 2 1

This is a work of fiction. Names, characters, places and incidents are either the
product of the author's imagination or are used fictitiously, and any resemblance
to any actual person, living or dead, events or locales is entirely coincidental.

ISBN 9789815017144

Typeset in Caslon by MAP Systems, Bangalore, India
Printed at Markono Print Media Pte Ltd, Singapore

www.penguin.sg

You know how it is. You pick up a book, flip to the dedication page, only to find that, once again, the author has dedicated a book to someone else and not to you. Well, not this time, folks. Maybe we haven't yet met, or perhaps we have but just had a glancing acquaintance in the past.

It matters not, as this one's for you. All of you. Every single one of you on the planet earth and beyond.

Contents

Author's Note

Firstly, thank you so much for buying, borrowing, lending or even, dare I think it? stealing a copy of this book from a friend. No matter the means of your getting your hands on a copy, thank you for preparing to read *Duxton Hill*. Who doesn't love a swoon-worthy romantic comedy, set around two loveable protagonists, dripping with humour and enough tension to keep you turning the pages? Assuming it has been well written, of course. Well, I can honestly state that I have given this book my every effort, bled ink and used only the good words. Writing a book is a marathon. It demands discipline and passion. All of which I have given freely in the pursuit of excellence. Perhaps writing is an art form that is never mastered, you just become a better student. It is then with the hope that I have become a better student that I present to you my brainchild in the form of this literary enterprise.

I feel like I have been in Clara's head for so long now! Clara is one of the main characters in this book through whose eyes we embark upon this adventure. The story is, of course, a work of fiction, but I hope that the scenes resonate with people and perhaps may even help in some way to understand life better. Locations and places used in the story are real, although monstrously misused by me to buzz up the atmosphere and add a little magic. For that, I hope

I am forgiven by the readers that live in these wonderful locations and places for any cheeky liberties I may have taken.

Thank you for your support!

Mark Powell
Author. 2021

The Duxton Hotel

The Duxton Hotel is a slightly rundown, sun-bleached and peeling-at-the-edges, yet charming structure, which now stands bookended by its newer neighbours. The Duxton, so named because it is situated on Duxton Hill, which nestles in the very heart of the historic island state of Singapore in a lively area within a short walking distance from the main metropolis. Duxton Hill is blessed indeed for it is surrounded by an array of picturesque churches, old-time shophouses, Buddhist temples, cafés and monuments to bygone years.

Upon entering the hotel, you will immediately sense its special, intimate, home-away-from home atmosphere. Each attention to detail has been passionately considered and each room deserves a visit. The style of the Duxton Hotel is a unique blend of valuable antiques and original, local artworks with an unexpectedly eclectic and contemporary twist. The entire hotel recalls the ancient flavours of times past when young Asian and European aristocrats lived in the region and revelled in the beauty and exotic mysteries of the East.

Sadly, the years of its existence are now starkly evident upon its façade, in its peeling paint and tired interiors. Like the guests who choose to stay within its walls, both past and present, we all age inevitably.

The Beginning

It may be the first conversation we will have. But I assure you this is not the last, because I'm about to share a story. It's rather long, so I want you to prepare yourself properly. It's a nice story, in my opinion, because it's a story about me. Having said that, it all depends on your point of view and your perspective of life. Are you an optimist or a pessimist? Depending on your personality, you may need a box of tissues to dab away some tears, or you may split your sides laughing at my misfortunes. You may even have no reaction at all, which would be kind of sad. No matter the outcome, it is my hope that your emotions are stirred in some form or other. So, with that said, make yourself comfortable and I shall begin.

I kept a diary up to the age of sixteen. Yes, sweet sixteen. The age at which my drunken father ran off with a married woman. He just upped and left one morning, with no explanation—not even a scribbled rant heaping blame in some form or another on someone or other. It was only when the cuckold came looking for my father a week or so after he had made himself scarce that Mum and I discovered that my ignoble papa had been having a sordid affair for years. Since that day, it has just been my mother and I.

I've looked back at the diary recently. I don't think it would be of any interest to anyone. If I were to leave it on a bus, or a burglar were to steal it from under my bed, they would see that within the cover I had written in bold letters with a thick, blue pen that a reward of $50 would be paid upon its safe return. Despite the promise of a reward, I'm not sure anyone would bother to take the trouble to collect the reward, much less start to read about me, unless, of course, one were interested in the ramblings of a socially inept, Singaporean girl with an obsessive compulsive disorder—and an almost fetish-level obsession for Ferrari-red lipstick.

I had an imaginary friend called Emily when growing up. She still makes an appearance now and then when I feel like talking to her. I was insecure, you see. I had panic attacks over acne and struggled with my tics and compulsions. It was no surprise that none of my romantic relationships ever lasted long. I was always a burden to my boyfriends, and they never took me seriously. My relationships invariably ended after a mere fortnight. I guess that explains what Loretta, my best friend and Singaporean sister at work, calls my 'boy-crazy' behaviour—that is, my tendency to overcommit, as a last-ditch attempt to cling to any guy who ever showed me even the least bit of interest. Perhaps my father's adultery when I was at a vulnerable age had something to do with it.

But I digress—back to my story. A couple of weeks ago, I was attending a hospitality job fair. I sat down just as the lights dimmed and the words 'Hospitality Career Opportunities' appeared on a large, cinematic screen in front of me. A colourful series of mouth-watering and jaw-dropping images followed, presenting Hong Kong, Tokyo, Bangkok and Phuket, Ubud in Bali and other exotic places, which would usually have me thinking wistfully about going on a vacation that I couldn't afford, but my trusty credit card could. But, on that specific day I couldn't relax, because reality had struck and I desperately needed to find a job. My bank account was almost at zero and the salary I earned helping at my uncle, Chin Wei's gym, was barely enough to cover my bus fare to work, let alone live off it. In any case, I couldn't focus on the presentation because of the frantic note taking of the zealous lady in the seat beside me as she simultaneously and vociferously interrupted the host with an incessant barrage of inconsequential questions. I did my utmost to ignore her, I really did. My loud tut-tutting and eye-rolling did little to dampen her enthusiasm. When the lights eventually came back on and we were invited to leave, I was handed a leaflet that everyone else seemed to ignore or treat like junk mail. But, having read it, and I'm forever glad I did, I smiled.

The Duxton Hotel was looking for a client-relations manager. So, with no further ado, I took out my phone and called the number on the leaflet.

No more than three hours later, my interview with the hotel's owner had ended and I had been completely bowled over and inspired by the quaintness of the Duxton area. I was seriously considering starting my diary again.

There's just one small fact I need to point out first: Duxton Hill, the area in which I was stood after the interview, reflecting at the time, is a minuscule hill. In all honesty, you could barely call it a hill at all, more a wondrous bump upon the urban landscape of the tropical island metropolis known as Singapore.

'The hill', as it is known to those of us who frequent it, which is now the go-to place for social outings, wining and dining, was once dreaded for its ruthless gangs that lorded over its brothels, opium dens and slums. Yet, despite its sinister and seedy past, it has risen through the ages to become an area of serene splendour, beauty, prestige and charm. Its vibrancy and sustainability as a local hotspot for food and culture is often seen as a reflection of the diversity of its past, as well as its future. Standing in its very centre, bearing the ravages of time with pride, is a hidden jewel of elegance, and the place I was now going to work at, the Duxton Hotel.

I owe a debt of gratitude to Ken, the quirky concierge, a man in his early thirties, of slight build and salon-styled hair, for having recounted the captivating story of this hotel to me before I became more intimately acquainted with it. His tale had such depth of detail that I felt I had been transported back in time to its heydays.

It begins in the once-grand lobby, peppered with fraying armchairs, faded teapoys and threadbare rugs that lie timelessly upon the black-and-white tiled floors, all of which yearn and hope to be restored one day. The lighting is too bright in places and too dim in others. In its midst, Ken stands sentinel, dressed in a black suit and looks like an abandoned mannequin as he reads a newspaper behind his desk. The other staff meander around like lobotomized zombies, all wearing the same blue-themed uniforms with gold piping. Their feeble attempts to look busy are snapped back to attention when an elderly Asian couple, the first guests in a while who are not seeking to 'rent a room by the hour' enter the hotel and now stand in the middle of the hotel lobby with the expectation of service, dripping water around their array of non-branded luggage.

The man is Tony Chan. He is understandably somewhat damp at the edges. He is short in stature with slightly rounded shoulders and snow-white, thinning hair. He presents a figure who would pose no physical threat to anyone. He could be anyone's favourite uncle or grandfather. Yet, beneath this comfortable, sixty-eight-year-old and well lived-in looking exterior, I am reliably informed, lies hidden the heart of a lion and a brain that could strip a balance sheet down to the cent in mere seconds.

He is grandmaster of the art of thick face, black heart—which means he could stab you in the heart with a blunt spoon, smiling sweetly at you all the while, and reassure you that there were no hard feelings. Such an act for him would be nothing more than business as usual. For any of you who have not read the book, entitled *Thick Face, Black Heart* by Chin-Ning Chu, I recommend it. It is something I need to practise more myself.

However, Mr Chan looks physically drained from his three-hour meeting earlier that day with a bunch of Chinese investors, the five-hour flight from Beijing and the somewhat bumpy, motion-sickness-inducing taxi ride from Changi Airport to the hotel. He is in sore need of rest. As does his petite wife of forty years, Pauline Chan. She stands beside him, shivering in the aircon, stoic and uncomplaining.

Anyone else happening upon the scene might think that the Chans were simply overseas guests checking in for a much-needed vacation, but all that Pierre Allard, a man too small to tolerate any form of criticism, a hypersensitive pimple of a human being and the hotel's general manager, sees from his post at the front desk, is an Asian couple in their silver-fox years, dressed very casually, dripping water on to his highly polished marble floor and Persian rugs. On the wall behind him is a portrait of the hotel's proud owner, Peter Lee.

Allard rushes out from behind the front desk as if he were on greased wheels and within seconds, stands looming over the Chans.

'Good evening, I'm Pierre Allard, the general manager. May I help you?' He speaks with a distinctive French accent, every word over-enunciated with perfect Parisian arrogance.

'Yes. Reservation under Chan,' Mr Chan replies, shaking the water from his jacket.

'I see. You are, I'm assuming, a Chinese national?' Allard enquires, eyeballing Mr Chan and taking in his old and now soaked brown, suede shoes and well-worn, grey, two-piece suit. Not one for flamboyance, Mr Chan is a man of practicality and humility, known for extracting every inch of wear out of anything he owned.

'I'm Singaporean Chinese to be exact. I grew up in this area,' Mr Chan responds. Allard pauses, resenting being set straight.

'I see. One moment, I will check your reservation,' Allard zooms back to his place behind the front desk, elbowing aside the timid, male, front-desk receptionist (Charles) and proceeds to tap away furiously on the computer keyboard.

'He appears a bit uptight, my dear,' Mrs Chan whispers to her husband.

'Yes. Indeed, he does.'

'Hmm,' Allard snorts. 'I have you down for the Duxton Suite, one of our finest rooms, for three nights. Is that correct?' Allard seems rather taken aback that this tiny and rather dishevelled couple now standing in his lobby can afford such a luxury room for a night, let alone three nights.

'Yes, that is correct,' Mr Chan confirms.

Far from convinced, Allard goes rigid and continues condescendingly, 'That suite is $900 per night, plus tax. Not, you understand, $900 for all three nights that you've booked?'

Pauline leans into her husband once again and loops her arm through his, 'Does he have any idea who we are, dear?'

'It begins as it must and it will end as it will, my dear,' Mr Chan replies, his face breaking into the sheepish half-smile normally reserved for when one passes wind in public. In case you are wondering how I know that, my mother does it all the time after eating eggs.

'Yes, I do know who you are. Chinese tourists,' says Allard, blightingly. 'I'll have to put you in a cheaper room then. Three hundred a night with two single beds is the best I can do,' Allard smirks, seemingly enjoying this masterly put down.

Mr Chan's posture stiffens, his face darkening, 'I would consider not doing that if I were you. We will take the suite and not pay a cent for it.'

Allard, now rendered almost speechless by Mr Chan's confident tone, splutters, 'Is this a joke? This is not a youth hostel.'

Before he can say another word, he freezes in his tracks, having suddenly caught sight of Peter Lee, the hotel's owner himself, emerging through the front doors and embracing Mr Chan like a long-lost friend.

'My dear, Tony. How long has it been now? Five years?' Mr Lee then embraces Mrs Chan with similar affection. 'Pauline. You look wonderful. A pearl of wonderment.'

Momentarily recovering, Allard says, 'Sir, do you know these people?'

Without even looking at Allard, Mr Lee replies, 'Don't just stand there, Ben show them up to the Duxton suite. My guests will wish to change into some dry clothes.' Lee clicks his fingers in the air and the hotel staff snap to attention and rush to gather up the Chans' luggage.

'But sir, I just—' Allard protests feebly.

'And Allard,' Lee continues dismissively, 'I entrust you to inform the staff of a very important announcement this evening: as of yesterday, my family's long history as custodians of the Duxton Hotel, from its nineteenth-century beginnings to this moment in time, has come to an end.'

Allard gapes in disbelief. 'What? This cannot be. No.'

'Oh, but it is so. I sold the hotel to my dear friends, the Chans. Incidentally, Mr Chan owns forty-three other hotels around the world. So, you are in very safe hands,' Lee concludes.

'I—I—' Allard gulps.

'Yes, these fine people are the new owners,' Lee takes Pauline's arm and strolls off towards the elevator. 'After you've changed and rested, time for some champagne, I think,' Lee waits for Mr Chan to join them.

Chan holds up a finger to indicate he needs a moment. He turns to face Allard, who is now looking ashen.

'Oh yes, I almost forgot,' Chan beams a patently fake smile and turns to Allard with the mien of a predator moving in for the kill. 'We have had many, many long months of struggle and of suffering. You may ask, what is my strategy? To which I reply: it is to wage war with all our might and all the strength that God can give us against a monstrous, dark and lamentable tyranny, never surpassed, in the catalogue of hospitality. That is my strategy. You ask, what is my aim? I reply with one word: Victory; victory at all costs; victory despite the competition; victory, however long and hard the road may be; for without victory, there is no survival.'

Chan pauses to observe Allard, who is dumbstruck. 'Oh. One last thing. I will no longer be needing your services, Mallard. Goodbye.'

'It's Allard, sir,' Allard tries to whisper.

'Yes, yes. Callard,' Chan having had his fun, follows his wife leaving Allard to stand rooted to the floor with the shock he had just received in the middle of the lobby.

Now, that's the history. As for how I, Clara Tan, factor myself into this story, you are about to find out. Should you see me in the street, you could always stop me and ask? I have shoulder length brown hair, cut into a neat bob. I'm 1.75 metres tall and have what my mum describes as a body tailormade to fashion Lululemon active wear. I think that is a compliment and means that I keep myself in shape. But I do feel my arms are too long for my body and my face a little sharp. Loretta says I look like a young Maggie Q. Anyway, before you do see me, I need to go and freshen my lipstick.

Chapter 1

It was a Saturday morning. A letter had arrived for me, and mother had placed it on the dining room table. I never received letters, only bills. So, you can imagine my excitement when I saw the envelope propped up against a mug of steaming hot camomile tea. I wasted no time in opening and reading it.

Flat 08-22,
423 Tiong Bahru Road,
Singapore

6 July 2018

Dear Ms Tan,

Congratulations! We are pleased to offer you the position of Client Relations Manager, subject to references and background checks.

We at the Duxton are proud of our heritage and have high expectations of you. We require all our staff to always be presentable, professional and ambassadors for our hotel chain.

Your starting salary will be $30,000 per year. You will be expected to work 40 hours per week.

Once again, congratulations! Do try not to have any further black eyes. However, please feel free to rearrange my pens whenever you like.

Yours sincerely,
Mr Tony Chan, Hotelier.

'But what if I were to suddenly die?' twang, twang. 'What if a tsunami wipes out the entire city of Singapore?' twang, twang. 'What if I'm sitting in the doctor's office and I involuntarily scream aloud?' twang, twang.

'Emily,' I said. Then, realizing that I had in fact just addressed my imaginary friend, I continued despite the irrationality, 'What do you think?'

I could hear her in my head, as clear as a bell, telling me not to be so defeatist and to enjoy the moment. And before you panic and summon a psychiatrist, I know Emily is not real. It just makes me feel better to call on her sometimes.

You see, for as long as I can remember, I, Clara Tan, now aged twenty-nine, have had these worrying thoughts. In fact, I've had these horrible, intrusive thoughts during the day, every day, and I twanged a red rubber band around my left wrist to break the traumatizing train of thought from progressing any further and reducing me to a gibbering wreck, just as someone might knock on wood when discussing a worst-case scenario. It was a weird thing to do, I agree, like excessively washing your hands or keeping your desk impeccably organized—which I also do, by the way. Also, I couldn't leave a room without checking my lipstick, which had to be a deep red. Fingernails and toenails didn't matter, but the lips had to be perfect—vampish and bright red. It was just one of those things my brain told me must be done. I assumed this was how it was for everyone?

My mother took me to see a doctor once; she said my behaviour was not normal. We've all heard it hundreds of times before: the trope of the germophobic, hygiene-obsessed person who was described as having OCD (an obsessive compulsive disorder).

And we've all heard people use the term 'OCD' to describe people who were pernickety or fastidious. People would probably say, 'Sorry, I'm just a bit OCD!' when they were picky about the alignment of their cutlery or books on a shelf. Well, it didn't matter, I was all of the above and proud of it. Proud because I lived with it, managed it and embraced it. Not that I went around with a sign around my neck blazoning the fact. Where would the fun be in that?

When people asked me what I did for a living—taxi drivers, strange men in bars, aunties at the bus stop—I told them politely that I worked at a hotel. In the two years that I had worked at the Duxton Hotel, no one had ever asked me what type of hotel the Duxton was—a boutique hotel or a nondescript part of a faceless franchise. Neither did they ask how many stars it had, or what specific job I did there. I couldn't decide whether that was because I perhaps fitted perfectly with the stereotype they had of a person who worked in a hotel, or because they didn't really care.

Perhaps they did care and understood perfectly well what a job in a hotel entailed and simply filled in the blanks for themselves. Maybe I changed bedsheets, or cleaned the toilet bowls, or helped with the checking-in of guests, or fought an ongoing battle with a photocopy machine in the back office, or perhaps just flipped omelettes at the breakfast station. Not that I ever complained. In fact, I was delighted when they did assume, as it meant I didn't have to explain the details.

As a matter of fact, I worked at the hotel's main reception desk and helped with guest relations, which meant I listened to a wide variety of guests' complaints, occasional compliments and ran the odd errand when a guest needed something from the nearby 7-Eleven when either Ken, the concierge, or Ben, the bellboy, was not available. I was always amazed at how specific the male guests were with the type of condom they needed: glow-in-the-dark, banana flavour or condoms designed with the thickness of the rubber as fine as a hair. Not that I paid much attention to the details on the packet and just grabbed anything that said Durex on the box.

When I first started working at the hotel, whenever anyone asked what I did, I told them I was middle management. But that backfired as they assumed I had more authority than I actually did. So, I changed my response to 'client-relations officer'. Their faces at that point tended to glaze over and I was treated as just another pretty face whose only skill they assumed was to smile and hand over a room key. I had been working here since I was twenty-seven.

Mr Chan, the owner of this little gem upon Duxton Hill, took me on not long after buying it and reopening it after a full renovation. I always thought he felt sorry for me. I did have a degree in English, but no work experience to speak of, unless you counted the four years of helping my uncle Chin Wei run a kick-boxing gym in Chinatown. The longer I worked there, the more complacent I had become, so I had quit because I needed the push to motivate me to get myself a decent job, and not one that held no future for me.

I had arrived for the interview with Mr Chan, sporting a black eye from my last round of kick-boxing and absent-mindedly straightened all the papers and pens on his desk. I specifically remember his intent observation of me as I did so. His eyes were warm and he offered a smile. A patient, grandfatherly smile that said he understood me. He just accepted what I was doing and didn't draw attention to my eccentricity or ask me to explain it. As for the black eye, could it be that perhaps he sensed courage? Either that or he felt that my ability to take a good beating would be a huge asset as the hotel's relationship manager. Whatever the reason for his hiring me, he watched over me from that day forward. He sat me down for long chats in the afternoon over pots of earl grey and told me about his childhood. I listened to him for hours as he talked about politics, music, investments, taxes, design, food and best of all, how to read people, of which I was clueless. He basically life-coached me.

Pauline, his lovely wife would join us sometimes and simply look on and smile, until one day, right out of the blue, she told me how desperately they had tried for a child of their own, but to no avail. It was as if I filled that void somehow. In a few short months we had become very close, and I looked upon them both with love and respect. They even paid for my mother to have surgery when she broke her ankle after falling off a footstool—she had been trying to reach for an old cake tin in which she saved lose change, for a rainy day on the top shelf.

I was treated well, despite the fact it was a two-tier system in the hotel—the essential staff and the family members. You could tell which people fell into which category as the Chans pushed the people who were considered family harder than the general staff. Because I was treated like family, I worked extra hard; I was paid well enough and wanted for nothing, but I did know that if I ever needed help, it would be unconditionally given. Not that I would have ever taken advantage of their generosity.

From Monday to Friday, I came in at 7.30 a.m. I took an hour's break for lunch. Initially, I brought my own food, until I was told to just order what I wanted from the kitchen.

I sat in the staff room, ate my lunch and read the *Straits Times* from cover to cover. I didn't talk to anyone because, by the time I had ordered, eaten my lunch and read the newspaper, my hour would be up. I realized I had no interest in fancy food. My preference was for cheap food with enough nutrients to keep me alive— basically anything quick and easy to prepare or buy, aside from my mother's homemade, black-chicken soup, of course, which is a treat and so delicious.

I then returned to the front desk and continued working until 9.00 p.m. When I got home, I washed, changed into silk pyjamas and read a book for an hour. This was my routine.

I always had a chat with my mum for an hour every evening. She would tell me about her day: trips to the wet market to buy fresh produce and who she met. She cleaned the house for a few elderly neighbours and made me laugh when she told me about old Mr Lee, an elderly neighbour in his eighties, who frequently passed wind, an odour so foul, as my mother described it, that the paint on the walls peeled. He would then wax lyrical about his time in the war and how he had evaded the Japanese by hiding in a sewer. I so loved our chats in the evening.

I went to bed around midnight, staring up at the ceiling and pondering life, but not before I had made sure everything in my room was in its place and perfectly aligned. I never had trouble falling asleep once I closed my eyes. I dreamed of meeting my white knight with whom I planned to have a family.

Every other Friday, I had the day off because I had to work on alternate Saturdays, so I took the bus to Orchard Road and window-shopped around the various high-end shopping malls. I tried on clothes and pretended I had an event to attend or a handsome date. It was sad in a way, but it made me feel better. Sometimes, I went into a bar, ordered a vodka and knocked it back in one. I would picture the look of sadness on my mother's face were she to discover I did that, because my runaway father had a drinking problem. Sometimes, I took two shots. It gave me a buzz, made me feel alive.

On Saturday mornings, I went kick-boxing at my uncle's gym. I followed a strict routine for three hours solid until I almost passed out. I then headed to work for the late shift. Sundays and every second Saturday, thankfully, were my days off.

My phone didn't ring often, but when it did, it made me jump— it was usually my mother or Mr Chan. Sometimes it was a cold caller wanting to sell me insurance or a gym membership.

'You've reached Interpol,' I would whisper. 'How can I help you?' The person would promptly hang-up and I would laugh on the inside.

I only had only one real friend while growing up, and that was Mary. But she had married young and moved to London. As such I didn't hear from her any more. Loretta had replaced her and was the closest thing I had to a best friend. We had become sisters almost.

I sometimes felt so tenuously connected to Earth that a strong gust of wind could rip me away and cast me into space like a dandelion seed at the mercy of the winds. The threads, which connected me to this earthly plane and gave me a purpose in life, got stronger and more substantive during my working week. People in the hotel needed me to check them in, upgrade their rooms, settle their accounts, make reservations, order flowers for their rooms and not tell their wives that they had checked in under an assumed name along with a woman who looked young enough to be their daughter.

I sometimes wondered if, for any reason, I wasn't standing behind the front desk, whether anyone would, in fact, notice my absence. It may occur to them that the brochures, offering tours to the various attractions around the island, were not as neatly arranged, or that the assorted red and green sweets in the glass jar on the check-in desk were not aligned by colour; but me, no, they wouldn't miss me. Loretta, the other receptionist, who was my friend, confidante and sister, and Ken would, I hoped. But Ben, the bellboy, I was sure, would most definitely not notice my absence, because he seemed to perpetually be in a reverie.

I could only hope that someone would call my mother or call at my home. I suppose someone would eventually call the police, wouldn't they? But considering that I've never taken a sick day, it would be most unlike me to not show up for work.

However, today was not the day that I would be vanishing off the face of the earth. I was seated on the number twelve bus, for which I was thankful as it had just started to rain. It was a miserable day, and everyone looked miserable, huddled in their raincoats, or sheltering under umbrellas. Rain in Singapore was frequent, being a tropical island. When it rained, people suddenly became grumpy and ill-tempered. I glanced out of the window and fogged the glass with my breath. The world looked back at me through the droplets of rain streaming down the window pane.

I had always taken great pride in managing my life, living with OCD, growing up with a single parent. After my father had absconded, Mum vowed to never remarry. She said to marry for a second time would be a solution to a problem she didn't have. She was happy being single and, like me, she was a survivor. I too was living my life on my own terms, but unlike her, I needed someone—there was a hole in my life, a missing part of a puzzle. I was not yet a self-contained entity. At least that is what I told myself every single day.

But today was going to be different. Something was about to happen. I could feel it in my water. I just didn't know what.

Chapter 2

I was on the late shift today and just a few stops away from the hotel, but the rain didn't seem like it was going to let up any time soon. The light outside was prematurely fading due to thick grey rain clouds moving in.

Now, if there was one essential purchase I wished I had made after leaving home, it would have been an umbrella. Instead, I had invested in a copy of the *Singapore Business Times*, which was not completely crazy as the *BT* was by far the best accessory a girl could have. Just think about it. Its major advantages were: it costed only a dollar and thirty cents; it could be used, as I discovered, as a makeshift umbrella; and if you walked into a room with it tucked under your arm, people took you seriously. You could banter about what was going on in the world. The rise and fall of the stock market, for example, and instead of thinking you were an airhead, people would think you were an intellectual chick who had a broader set of interests, other than shoes. Not that it had stimulated much conversation for me over the past forty minutes. I was now pressed up against a man with very poor standards of personal hygiene on a bus. To make matters worse, despite my copy of the *Business Times*, I was not feeling like a power chick; I was feeling old and dowdy in my hotel uniform. Yet, little did I know that I would soon be strangely thankful that it was raining.

As I reached the steps leading up to the main entrance of the hotel, I saw him, washed up, not like a drowned rat or a singular flip-flop that you sometimes saw on the pavement, but a man, a real, red-blooded man. At least, I assumed he was red-blooded. He could turn out to be a wimp. But for now, I would allow my imagination free rein. He was pleasant enough to look at, well dressed, with moss-green eyes and sported the fashionable stubble. But that wasn't what drew my attention. No, it most definitely wasn't. It was the fact that he was wiping his feet on the doormat before stepping through the revolving door into the main lobby. A true gentleman always wiped his feet before entering a home. At least that was what the Earl of Grantham said on *Downton Abbey*. Nevertheless, to me it was a sign to look out for, signifying as it did that he had good manners, something so many men seemed to lack these days.

He looked sophisticated, elegant and a man with the appropriate qualities that I should seek. He was about my age at least. He had a handsome Caucasian face, his voice was deep and manly as he said 'hello' to the doorman and the most important point of all, he gestured for me to enter the revolving doors first . . . I gave my rubber band a twang to make sure I wasn't dreaming, then allowed my eyes to rest upon him for a moment longer. Yes, he could be a man who could be described with some degree of certainty as 'boyfriend material'. You see, I couldn't help myself—here was a man not even a minute old in my tiny world and I was already hearing wedding bells. My momentary flight of fancy was thankfully broken as he spoke.

'Please, after you,' he said, in what I detected to be a polished English accent. I took another pause to absorb him. He was British?

This meant yet another thing I had learnt from binge-watching the *Downton Abbey* episodes back-to-back: he could switch at will between being uptight and arrogant to being funny and wryly self-deprecatory.

But never mind that now, *twang*. I swear to God, if I twanged my rubber band any harder it would snap. I needed to calm down.

He stood in the entranceway to the Duxton Hotel shaking the wetness from his well-tailored, gold-buttoned, navy-blue blazer before combing the fingers of a hand through a mop of brownish hair and pushing it away from his forehead. It was, without doubt, a sign from the gods. I remember Ken telling me that, when the Chans bought the hotel, they had been caught in a sudden downpour as well. Now here was this rain-soaked man in Duxton, probably a harbinger of great change.

It then occurred to me that he seemed lost. Lost as in physically lost, not lost in mind, you understand. I deduced from the fact that he had no luggage with him, that he couldn't be a guest at the Duxton. He probably wasn't meeting anyone in the hotel either because he would have checked his watch and directly rushed in. That is, unless he was James Bond and being very cool. Safe to say he wasn't a British spy on a mission to save the world. No, he was just hanging around; looking for something.

He smiled pleasantly just then, tiny dimples playing peek-a-boo on his cheeks. 'I thought it only rained like this in England,' he said, as he again gestured for me to precede him through the revolving door. I thought he was charming.

I wiped my feet on the doormat thrice as always and stepped through the door. As I passed by him, I confess I smiled, not that he would have noticed. However, he did notice the damp, drooping-at-the-edges copy of the *BT* in my hand. He followed me through the revolving door as it started to rotate. As you are probably aware, each quadrant of the revolving door is not really designed to house two people at a time. So, here I was, pressed up against a stranger, for a second time this day, albeit a handsome one.

'Anything interesting?' he asked. I looked up at him pretending I didn't understand the question.

'Sorry?' I prompted. We had completed a couple of revolutions already, going past the lobby doors twice and seemed to have gotten into an endless spin cycle.

'The newspaper you have there. I wondered if there was anything interesting in it?' He tried to point with a finger, but the limiting confines of the space didn't make it easy. Was I really having this conversation in a revolving door? We were now on our third revolution.

'Oh. Yes. It has an article titled, "It didn't start with you", by Mark Wolynn,' I replied with a smile. I should have stopped there, but my mouth seemed to have a mind of its own and decided to run off with my brain trailing behind reluctantly. 'It's about people with OCD and how past trauma may cause the condition.' I couldn't seem to be able to stop now, 'I like to learn everything I can about it.'

Now that would have sounded very weird to most people. I thankfully fell silent at that point, but it was too late for me to retract my words.

He responded in a friendly tone, 'Fascinating.' Which, of course, I took to mean he didn't find it interesting at all.

At long last, Ben stopped our ride by grabbing the door and bringing us to an abrupt halt. We had now been deposited back outside the main entrance and were both a little embarrassed.

'Do you have OCD?' I asked conversationally. Now, why would I ask him that, a complete stranger at that? At least I hadn't divulged to him that I did. That would have been a bit much to share with a stranger.

His response didn't surprise me, 'No, I don't. I'm Nicholas by the way, Nicholas Tate. My friends call me "Nick".' He extended his hand but, like a complete flake, I had become too lost in his words to notice. I suddenly snapped back to reality, jerked out a hand and shook his hand peremptorily. I should have allowed the touch to linger.

'I'm Clara. Clara Tan,' I blurted out. 'And I like the name Nicholas, so if it's all right with you, I'll not shorten it.'

'Fair enough. Well, it's very nice to meet you, Clara Tan,' he replied along with another bone-melting smile.

'Work here, yes. Here at the hotel. Can I help you?' My words just tumbled out in no logical order. He must have concluded that I was very weird by now. So, I tried again, 'I work here at the hotel as the guest-relations manager. Can I help you with anything?' I could feel him looking at me intently. He was absorbing me like a sponge does water, and most likely wondering why he was bothering at all with this gauche woman.

It seemed like an eternity before he spoke again, 'Well, you could point me in the direction of a good whisky while I wait for this damn rain to stop and, if I'm honest, I am lost.'

So I was right after all. He was lost.

'Oh, lost,' I repeated.

'Yes. I'm new in town. I've been wandering around for half an hour now, trying to find my way back to Baker and Oakley. It's an advertising agency on Amoy Street. Silly, really . . . I took a stroll to clear my head and explore the surroundings, got hopelessly lost in the narrow alleyways, then got caught in the sudden downpour and here I am, lured by the warm, inviting glow from the street-side windows of your hotel.'

I took this all in slowly, then replied, 'Yes, of course. Our bar is just through there, to the left. They have some excellent Scotch whisky, twenty years, aged.' I gestured to indicate the direction of the bar.

'You know your whisky,' he said.

'Part of my job, I guess. I do like the odd glass on occasion' I replied.

'Thank you, Clara. You're very kind,' he replied, before proceeding through the revolving door again. Only this time alone. I followed. Just before entering the bar which was just a few yards away, he turned back to look at me to see if I had moved.

I was still rooted to the spot like a deer caught in the headlights of an incredibly good-looking car. He shot me a smile before he disappeared through the doorway. I so badly wanted to follow him, but it would seem too obvious, not to mention, creepy. I turned around on the spot, twice, like a frantic cat chasing its own tail, dithering about what to do next.

I could feel the anxiety building up and headed towards the front desk. A rack of tourist pamphlets was about to be rearranged to abate my emotions. As I shuffled them skilfully like a croupier would a pack of cards and placed them back in the rack in perfect alphabetical order, which was the order in which they had probably already been, I noticed Loretta and Ken eyeing me.

The pair of them were like eagles, they missed nothing. Loretta didn't say anything, she didn't have to, her wry smile said it all, but I could tell she had observed Nicholas and the fact that I was flushed a bright shade of pink. Having gotten to know Loretta over the past few months, I knew that she could sniff out an eligible male, like a shark could, a drop of blood in the water.

'Not sure what you mean, Loretta. I have work to do. He's just passing through, not even a guest here. Not that you . . . I . . . would fraternize with a guest or a man I don't even know,' I think I was speaking more to myself than to Loretta.

'I didn't say a word, but should you want to go and see if he's settled in at the bar, I can cover for you. If not, I'll go.'

'Is every man fair game to you?' I snapped.

'If he can walk on his own two legs, is under the age of sixty-five, has a pulse and his own teeth then, yes,' she laughed.

'He's most likely married, or his girlfriend is some leggy Brazilian model who waxes every other day to ensure a silk scarf would slide off her every body part,' I waited for Loretta to respond. She shot me a look that confirmed I had lost the plot. Not really sure why I had thought of waxing.

'No,' she agreed. 'He's most definitely single. A mama's boy is my guess, and he sleeps on the right side of the bed,' she gave me a look that silently dared me to contradict her.

'I agree,' Ken joined in.

'Really? A mama's boy?' I've often wondered from where she drew such conclusions.

'Well, the only way to settle this is for one of us to go in there and find out. Come on, we have nothing better to do, the place is dead. I'll count to ten and if you don't go, I will,' Loretta's tone was decidedly final.

'I can't. It's against the rules to fraternize with the guests.' A pathetic excuse, I knew.

'One . . . two . . .' Loretta began to count.

'Aiyah,' Ken said in his best Singlish, 'it takes thirty seconds of courage to change your life, and those thirty seconds could map out your destiny, lah. You have never looked better, so get in there, girl, right now.'

Wow, I thought, Ken sounded assertive for once.

'. . . four . . . five . . .' Loretta was still counting.

I checked my lipstick in the mirror which I had secreted behind the desk and headed to the bar. But wait . . . what was I doing? This was insane!

Still on autopilot, I turned on my heel and beelined to the reception desk. I had barely taken two steps before Loretta raised a flat-palmed hand like she was a school-crossing guard and halted me in my tracks.

'Go! Now!' she said. Something snapped inside of me then. I've no idea why, but it did, and my mood flipped to waspish instantly.

'I'm not like you, Loretta, a human hop-on hop-off bus, with another man hopping on every five minutes.' An awful stillness ensued. It was as if someone had just died. No sooner than the words were out of my mouth that I regretted it. Too late. Loretta had already turned and walked away, stopping for a moment to look back at me with an expression like she had been sideswiped by a wet fish. I caught Ken flash her a reassuring look.

'That was uncalled for,' he said angrily, before stalking off as well.

Finding myself alone and guilt-ridden, I decided I might as well go in search of Nicholas, the new arrival from England.

As I entered the bar, I was still thinking about poor Loretta, she had looked so hurt. I vowed to apologize to her the moment I saw her next. But now, I needed to find Nicholas. I did a quick scan of the room. I could see two men, both in their late twenties, seated by the window, leaning into each other's conversation. No, not him . . . or him. Next a professional-looking couple who occupied a table in the centre of the bar. The woman, slender, Asian, in her forties, dressed in a blue suit, looking very corporate, yet sexy, caught my eye. I noticed her sleek, black hair was neatly styled to fall just above her shoulders, exposing the back of her slender neck. I wished I looked as elegant as her right now, instead of a stuffy, old woman in a hotel uniform. The man she was with, full-bellied, balding, in a grey suit was not Nicholas either. Thankfully.

Suddenly, I spotted him. He was seated alone, perched on a stool at the far end of the bar counter, nursing a whisky and checking his phone. I sidled up until I was standing right next to him.

'Erm—'

Nicholas looked up. 'You had me at hello earlier,' he said with a boyish smile.

'Sorry . . . hello?' I was a bit slow on the uptake and completely missed the delivery of what was clearly a cheesy, chat-up line.

'I wondered if you would come in to see me. And I'm very glad that you did,' he said.

'I wondered if I could help you further. You mentioned that you were lost?'

'Yes, I did, didn't I? Well, I was lost, but thanks to Google here, I now know, exactly to the meter, where I am. I work in Amoy Street. Which Google tells me is in that direction. A half-mile away to be exact,' he pointed.

'More like a mile actually,' I felt compelled to challenge Google.

'Right. Well, there you have it, then. Clara Tan is now officially replacing Google,' he chuckled. This was where I let myself down further, perhaps I was still upset over my rudeness to Loretta, or I was entering my period of PMT.

Clearly, I had lost my sense of humour, 'Sorry, I don't think that was funny. I was trying to help you,' I felt myself stiffen and a cold sweat broke out over me. My emotions do that and I hated how mercurial my moods could be.

'Easy, tiger, no offence intended,' he offered an easy smile to melt the frost forming on my frowning face.

'Well, you're a little way off Amoy Street,' I tried to recover my poise and pointed in the general direction of where he needed to be.

'Thank you. Care to join me for a drink?' he patted the stool beside his.

'No, but Emily can.' I dropped my head. Why on earth did I just say that?

'Emily?'

'Yes, Emily, my imaginary friend. You see, I can't, I'm sorry. I'm on duty. Rules are rules.' I thought honesty was the only way out of that embarrassing blunder. It made it seem almost appropriate to explain who Emily was, as he may think I was being cute, rather than insane.

'Yes, of course. Silly of me to ask. But yes, Emily is most welcome to join me,' he responded. He took a sip of his whisky and savoured it before swallowing. 'Hmm. Very nice, single malt.' He clearly felt the need to inform me or impress me. Not sure which.

'Well, enjoy it, and don't get Emily too drunk,' I replied with a smile and turned to leave. A hand then gently grabbed my wrist. My breath caught in my throat and I timidly glanced over my shoulder at Nicholas.

'Let's start again, shall we? How about you educate me on what exactly a guest-relations manager does? I'd love to know.'

'Really?'

'Yes, really.'

'Why?'

'Because, if I better understand what you do, I can add that to my knowledge bank and ensure that, should I ever run into you again, I respect what you do, as I should. You kindly offered to help me.' Clearly, he was very articulate and smooth.

'Well, I check-in guests mainly. Help them if something is wrong with their room or booking. Or, as is often the case, just listen to them moan and complain.'

'I see,' he took another meditative sip of his whisky. 'So, basically you babysit them,' he said smiling.

'Yes, I suppose I do,' I felt myself relaxing. 'And you?'

'Marketing. Basically. I identify customer needs and how best to satisfy them without their realizing that I'm steering them in an entirely different direction.' He tapped his glass with a finger, indicating to the barman that he wanted another.

'Direction? But aren't you the one who is lost?' I couldn't help but laugh.

'Very good. Sharp and witty, I see,' he said, but his slight frown seemed to suggest that he was either no longer in the mood for playful banter or he just didn't relate to my sense of humour.

'Thank you,' I replied, feeling slightly guilty.

He then gestured for the bill and stood up. 'I should let you get back to work. But it was very nice meeting you, Clara.' I looked at him, wondering why the sudden change in mood, and he had just ordered another whisky.

'Is something wrong? You didn't finish your whisky and it is a single malt,' I tacked on, trying to read his face.

'No. I'm fine. Really. It's just that I remembered I have some work to do back at the office. Besides, my bosses don't pay me to sit around chatting to women.'

'Women?' I repeated. Something about his tone felt belittling and offensive.

'Yes, women. You are a woman, aren't you?'

Was he now challenging my gender? I felt myself bridle and flush.

'Yes, I am a woman; a woman who tried to help you, remember? You were lost.'

Nicholas stiffened, 'Yes. So you keep reminding me. That joke is getting almost as old as the whisky.'

'Well, you could always leave,' I snapped.

'Yes. Perhaps I should,' he replied coldly. I busied myself tidying the coasters and glasses on the bar counter as a way of counterbalancing my spiralling anxiety. I could see him watching me. I was verbally jousting with a man I barely knew.

But there was something about him I liked—even though I had only just met him. I had been so sure that we had been hitting it off. What had gone wrong? This was so weird. I couldn't even remember what it was I had come in here to find out now. I paused, thinking hard for a moment.

'Mama's boy!' I ejaculated out of the blue. Now I had really done it. Everybody in the bar was staring at us. Not least, Nicholas who was glaring at me now.

'I beg your pardon?'

'Nothing. I was just . . .' I had no idea why I had said that or how to explain myself.

'I see. It would be best if I run off to find Mummy, then. I'm sure she is wondering where I am. After all, its past my bedtime,' he stormed off towards the lobby.

As I emerged a few moments later, I saw him standing a few feet from Ken. And, *oh God*, Loretta was behind the desk. I hadn't seen her since the insult. I needed to say something.

I approached the desk. 'Loretta, I'm so sorry, I shouldn't . . .' She silenced me with a finger across her own lips.

'Say no more, babe. Besides, don't you have something more important to deal with?' she flicked her eyes towards Nicholas in a meaningful glance.

'Take a seat, sir. I'll flag a taxi for you, although it may be a while with this rain,' Ken gestured to one of the plush, red, velvet armchairs. They were the kind of chairs you could sink into with a good book and a pipe, and not stir for days.

'Thank you,' Nicholas proceeded to make himself comfortable. I couldn't leave it like this; I needed to do something. Within the past half hour, I had offended two people. I decided to approach him.

'Will you be okay?' I asked.

'Yes, just fine, thank you,' he said breezily and with just a hint of sarcasm. 'I rather enjoy being lost.' I remained tight-lipped.

'Amoy Street is just a few minutes away, sir,' Ken interjected, having read some hostility in to his body language. We must have looked like two alley cats about to claw each other's eyes out. 'Are you staying long in Singapore, sir?' Ken interposed again.

'Not sure now, to be honest. Wasn't expecting frost in the tropics,' Nicholas responded, seeing I was within earshot.

'Working here, sir, or just passing through?' Ken continued his stock-in-trade catechism.

'Working. I'm over from London to run our Singapore office. I'm in advertising.'

I couldn't help myself as my mouth engaged again, 'I thought you said marketing?'

His eyes, now cold, 'Advertising is the exercise of promoting a company and its products or services through paid channels. In other words, advertising is a component of marketing. I do both.' He surveyed lobby.

'This place could use some resuscitating. Some new and original thinking?'

'Sounds very good, sir. I wish you well,' Ken smiled politely as he attempted to terminate the conversation and thereby put an end to our gibes.

'Thank you. By the way, Ken, if I were to go out for a good meal and some nightlife, where would I go?'

'Local nightlife, sir?'

'Yes. I suppose so,' Nicholas replied.

Before Ken could respond, I cut in, 'I would recommend Orchard Towers. It's on Orchard Road. Just ask any taxi driver. That way you won't get lost. And the people there are all advertising experts. Charge by the hour. Much like you, I suspect.'

Ken's smile now looked forced. 'I don't think sir would—'

'Has the taxi arrived, Ken?' I interrupted him and he turned to peer out through the window.

'Looks like it has just pulled up. Yes.'

'Nice to have met you all,' said Nicholas, 'it was . . . well, different.'

* * *

'Clara!' Ken expostulated. 'Orchard Towers. Really?'

I turned away in shame. I knew very well that I had gone beyond the pale.

'What has gotten into you, Clara? What did the poor guy ever do to you?' Loretta whispered.

'You're right. I'm not sure what happened to me. I really thought for a moment there that we were hitting it off.' I buried my face in my hands.

'Never mind, Clara. I don't think you'll ever see him again after today,' consoled Loretta and then thumped Ken on the arm.

'Ouch.'

'Ken!' Loretta hissed.

Ken stepped forward to attend to a lady in high-waisted jeans and a bright, purple t-shirt that screamed a feminist slogan. It was obvious that she was an American tourist.

Chapter 3

The three days that followed that rainy day passed very slowly. Apologizing to Loretta for likening her to a bus, had been easy, but I still felt deeply remorseful about what I had said to her. I continued to apologize and make it up to her as sincerely as I could.

The slow, dull days at the hotel I hoped would soon be over. We needed guests to stay open. It was time to wake up and get some positive motivation going among the staff. Why? Because, as I walked through the lobby of the hotel, I could tell that the imminent arrival of the Chans at the Duxton was upon us. The flurry of activity was normal whenever the Chans announced they would be coming to stay, as it triggered a ceremony, not unlike the one that would befit the arrival of the queen of England. Anything that could be polished to a mirror sheen, was. Floors were scrubbed and buffed until every speck of dirt had been removed. The carpets were shampooed and their pile restored. Drapes were dry-cleaned and uniforms, pressed. Every knife, fork and spoon was hand-washed and polished. Each piece of linen was starched and folded into neat squares. Nothing was left untouched. This was his expectation and the absolute minimum standard he expected from every one of his hotels. Unfortunately, it was not enough. The chatter on the rival hotel grapevine that passed between the concierges and bellhops was that the bookings at the Duxton were at an all-time low. The staff were rightly concerned as the gossip began to manifest, evidenced by the vacant rooms.

The day of the Chans' arrival only substantiated one's worst fears. Seeing everyone gathered together in the main function room, was far from normal. Every cook, chef, housekeeper, dishwasher, accountant, driver, maintenance man, bellhop, concierge and receptionist was there. All lined up like soldiers on parade. Silence reigned as the Chans entered and seated themselves.

'What's this all about?' Loretta whispered in my ear.

'I have no idea.'

'I hear he's gone bankrupt,' Ken stage-whispered from my other side causing those within earshot to gasp. I elbowed him sharply in his ribs, and he emitted a loud yelp, which made the Chans sit up and peer anxiously in our direction, worried that someone was in pain.

Charles Hong, the hotel's general manager, stepped forward. He was a tall, slender man, with hawk-like features and shiny, jet-black hair. He didn't so much walk as seemed to glide on a cushion of air. He had served the Chans loyally for twenty years and was by nature traditional, conservative and a stickler for convention and perfection.

I watched him rub the tiger's-eye beads that he wore on his right wrist, then stiffen in readiness to speak, 'Mr Chan has something he would like to say to you all. Please be attentive and hold any questions to the end. Thank you.'

Tony Chan got to his feet. Something wasn't right. His normally happy face looked defeated. His shoulders drooped and he wasn't excitedly rubbing his hands together as he usually did. His hands simply hung at his sides. I wanted to rush over to him and give him a warm embrace. Instead, I was rooted to the spot. And then, he began to speak.

'We are under attack,' he announced. He sounded stressed out.

Everyone looked around nervously like they expected to see a gang of masked men holding guns. Murmurs, inaudible at first, grew louder until Hong bellowed, 'Silence, please. Silence!'

The room fell silent, and Mr Chan continued, 'Our competitors are coming for us. They're stealing our guests, luring them with free weekend breaks, bus tours, cheap soaps and rooms that have less atmosphere than a prison cell.' Mr Chan paused, 'It seems people like this sort of thing. If this persists, we will not be able to survive.'

Murmurs erupted again. 'Quiet!' hollered Hong.

'You want us to be quiet,' one of the braver chefs spoke up from the back of the room, 'but what does this all mean?' Only the top of his chef's hat was visible above the crowd. The murmurs swelled again.

'Quiet. I said be quiet. Listen to Mr Chan, please!' Hong was now waving his arms around.

'We all have families to feed,' shouted another member of staff.

'Are we out of our jobs?' came another cry.

'I said be quiet . . . be quiet!' Hong was now gliding around on his cushion of air, shouting.

My anxiety levels had spiked as well by now. The decibel level in the room was now unbearably high. Palms sweating, pulse racing, mouth dry, rubber band twanging, I was jostled about and I felt as if I was standing in a swarm of bees. God, I felt terrible.

My thoughts then turned to the Chans. How terrible must they feel seeing us all lose the plot like this. I determinedly clamped down on the rising sense of panic within me and tried to find Ken and Loretta. I had to do something, but what? Loretta and Ken were nowhere to be seen. It was as if they had been swept away by an angry sea. I felt someone barge into my side as one of the kitchen staff pushed past me. I covered my ears, closed my eyes and willed my body to move; it was shutting down.

No, Clara, I psyched myself up. You must do something, anything.

I counted slowly backwards, 'Ten, nine, eight, seven . . .'

My heart pounded as I counted down. I could feel my heartbeat gradually slow down. I opened my eyes as it came to me and I suddenly knew exactly what to do.

A loud *Bongggg, Bonggggg, Bongggg* rang out and everybody fell silent. Amazed at how effective it had been, I felt immensely pleased with myself. That is until heads started turning in my direction.

I was standing isolated and alone at the back of the room clutching a large, bronze gong, looking sheepish at being the cynosure of all eyes. Even Hong had nothing to say. His mouth had fallen open, his eyes blazing. I had to say something.

'Ermmm. I . . .' I stuttered. I could feel the warmth emanating from my face. Across the room, the sea of people parted like the biblical Red Sea. The Chans were looking directly at me, as was everyone else. I could feel myself wilting like a weed in the hot sun.

'This is it,' I thought, 'I'll be fired for sure today.'

But just as I was about to wet myself and freak out completely, I saw the hint of a smile appear on his face. He gave me a thumbs up.

A surge of courage washed over me. That smile had made all the difference. It felt wonderful as if several shots of tequila, all at once, had flooded my veins. I then spotted Loretta on the periphery, giving me a thumbs up as well.

I dredged up my voice from somewhere down in my shoes. 'Can we please all calm down and listen to what Mr Chan has to say? We all owe him that, don't we?' I paused. 'We are acting like frightened children. Do we not have faith in the man who has treated us like family?'

'You're right, Clara,' Loretta piped up. 'At the first sign of trouble we panic. This is not who we are. Our first response should be to ask how we can help the Chans.'

'Okay, can everyone please sit down now?' Hong stepped forward and snatched the gong and gavel out of my hands. Just as he did, something very unexpected happened. A gradual applause, triggered by Loretta, rippled around the room. It was followed by another, and another, growing louder and finally erupting into a full-scale ovation. I couldn't believe it. As the cheering died down, Mr Chan and Pauline stepped forward.

'With this type of leadership, we will succeed. Now, the reason I gathered you all here today, is because . . . I wanted to ask you all for help and ask each and every one of you how we can change, adapt and conquer to beat the competition.' Chan paused. There was pin-drop silence. He then waved Hong over to join him at the front of the room.

'This man has served me well for the past twenty years, having worked in many of my hotels.' Hong stiffened and then for the first time ever, I saw him smile. I noticed that Loretta was rolling her eyes. 'This man has never failed me. He has done a great job in managing this hotel, post it's renovation.'

People started to grow fidgety again. It was obvious to all that Hong was about to get some sort of an award for his services. Loretta eased into the seat beside me.

'D'you think old man Chan will name a hotel after him?' she whispered in my ear and giggled.

Meanwhile, Mr Chan was still holding forth, 'The time has now come for my friend to pass the baton to the next generation, as he has announced to me his wish to retire.' The murmuring started up once again but was abated by the simple expedient of a wave of Mr Chan's hand. 'Please, please, I need just one more moment of your time so I can announce the appointment of a new GM.'

Everyone fell into a dazed silence, curious to know who would replace Hong.

'So, who is the new GM?' the same chef who had started the earlier furore spoke up.

'I shall tell you. It is someone I greatly respect and will work with you all to ensure our success for our combined futures.' He took a moment. 'Clara, please join me here, would you?' Mr Chan waved me over. I mechanically obeyed him. 'I want you to be the new GM, Clara.' He hugged me affectionately. I was delighted and honoured of course, if not a little in shock. But in a world of pandemics and climate change, sometimes good things do happen. Pauline then joined in. My world was now running in slow motion as I took it all in. All I could hear was applause.

An hour later, I had extricated myself from my well-wishers, the doubtful platitudes of my not-so-well-wishers and the baleful glare of Hong, to splash my face with cold water in the restroom.

I looked at my reflection in the mirror. I didn't see a general manager but a rather frightened young woman. A shudder ran through me. Two years as a front-desk clerk. Almost to the day, I realized. Happy anniversary, I thought to myself. Although my mother always told me to follow my dreams, I wasn't overly ambitious; yet, here I was, a GM for a luxury, boutique hotel. I felt a brief pang for Hong. It was my day today; not his.

I emerged from the restroom thirty minutes later and headed for Mr Chan's office. As I sat down, I noticed that a tray of earl grey tea and biscuits had been made ready.

'I have no words,' I managed to at least say that much, despite still being in shock. I looked at Mr Chan and took in his comforting smile.

'You're like a daughter to us, Clara. Both Pauline and I feel that what you did in there showed real courage and demonstrated to us that you are ready to lead.' He smiled at his wife sweetly.

'Yes, dear,' said Pauline. 'You have our support. Now I will leave you both to discuss business.' Pauline kissed me on the cheek and left the office.

Mr Chan leaned forward. 'Our enemy, my dear, is Baker Oakley. The young man that leads them is smart, forward-thinking and, I'm told, an expert in his field. He is leading a marketing push for our main competitor.'

I racked my brains to try and remember where I had heard that name before. Baker Oakley.

'Clara?' Mr Chan snapped me back.

'Yes, I'm listening,' I wasn't really, but I leaned in to show that I was now.

'We need to reinvent our brand or find something unique to offer our guests. This is the way forward.' Chan sat back.

'Yes. I agree,' I nodded.

'Good. We will need our A-game to beat this young man,' Mr Chan rubbed his hands together with excitement.

'This young expert man you mention, do you know him?' I asked.

'No. I hear he's just about your age and a real marketing gem.'

Now I was confused and my alarm signals were going off. This all sounded too familiar . . . then my stomach knotted.

Surely . . . it couldn't be. The word 'marketing' ricocheted inside my head. Impossible! The world has millions of young men in marketing, why would I think it could be . . . Before I could formulate his name in my head, Mr Chan confirmed the worst.

'His name is Nicholas Tate. An Englishman. Despite his youth, he has turned other hotel brands around the world into award-winning venues I am told,' Chan sighed.

'Nicholas?' I exclaimed.

'D'you know him?' Mr Chan looked almost as shocked as I was now.

'No. I mean . . . yes. He was here a few weeks ago.' I started to pace the room.

'He was here? Why?' Mr Chan looked concerned.

'No. He wasn't here to spy. He was lost in the rain. I—I, spoke to him. But only briefly.' I took a seat and started to rearrange the pens on his desk.

'Maybe he was just checking us out,' Mr Chan sounded suspicious.

I also began to wonder if his arriving at our doorstep like a drowned rat was just a ploy.

'Have you seen him since?' Mr Chan asked.

'No, I haven't.'

Mr Chan had the annoying knack of reading me like a book. 'Sit down, Clara, and tell me everything.'

I sat down. 'Not much to tell, really. It was raining and he said he was lost. So, I invited him in for a drink at the bar. As soon as the rain let up, Ken called him a taxi.'

'So, he didn't ask anything about the hotel?'

'No. Not that I recall.'

'Are you sure, Clara?'

'I think so, yes. He was rather charming though.'

Mr Chan smiled. 'Then we must use that as leverage. First rule of business, use what assets you have to best effect.'

'Sorry?'

'The law of attraction, Clara. You can use his interests in you to help us. It may not be ethical, but I'm sure you understand.'

'I still don't follow, sorry.' I was beginning to feel stupid and felt that perhaps I wasn't up to being GM after all. I reached for my rubber band, forgetting that it had snapped and yet to be replaced.

'You must track him down and convince him to help us. Not be the competition. Use your natural charm, Clara, for all our sakes.' Mr Chan was capitalizing on my affection for him. I guess that was why Mr Chan was a billionaire, and I was, well, just me. He knew how to take advantage of opportunities when they presented themselves.

'Clara, are you still with me?' Mr Chan brought me back to the topic at hand.

'Yes. I'm listening.' I remembered how my first encounter with Nicholas had ended. Not great, you would say and that would be an understatement.

Mr Chan then spoke: 'To cite *Julius Caesar*, "There is a tide in the affairs of men which, taken at the flood, leads on to fortune; Omitted, all the voyage of their life is bound in shallows and in miseries."'

I could tell that in his mind the solution had been found. The only problem was that the enormous weight of it now rested on my slim shoulders. I shuffled back to the front desk, my mind in overdrive. How would I find him again? Wouldn't he be back in London now? Even if I did find him, would he even speak to me? So many questions and as of now . . . no answers.

Chapter 4

There are crazy days and then there are just insane days. Yesterday was an insane day considering the mission Mr Chan had assigned to me. I don't think I slept for even a second last night and my body was now wilting. It was now early afternoon and I had been stuck behind my desk for hours, still mulling over the inevitability of having to face Nicholas within this week—that is, if I could track him down.

Another thing you should know about me is that I was level headed, more sensible than careless and I wasn't known to throw myself willy-nilly into the path of danger. Not that my life was in danger per se, but situations in which I didn't have control were situations I tended to steer clear of—as I reminded myself this repeatedly. So, how exactly did I end up in this predicament?

Well, I guess you could say it was all because I decided to engage in a childish game with Ken. We often played this game when things were quiet. The game required no words and it was very immature. One of the players simply mimed someone's facial expression and mannerisms. If any of the other players guessed right, then that player took over the miming. If a player made three wrong guesses, that player got to buy lunch. Ken began. He frowned and pouted. Too easy, I thought.

'Colin, the head chef.'

I was obviously right and Ken scowled in disappointment. My turn. I slouched, squinted with one eye and my face contorted into a grimace akin to someone who had accidentally sat on a spike. Ken shook his head. I sucked in my cheeks slightly to enhance my agonized expression.

'Lilly.'

'Correct.' I confirmed. Lilly was one of the room-service maids, whose features were permanently set in an anguished expression.

We continued the game for another fifteen minutes, or so. It did take my mind off things. That was until Ken decided to impersonate Nicholas, running his fingers through his hair and pretending to wipe his shoes on a non-existent doormat. Although it looked more like a lame impression of Michael Jackson's moonwalk, I immediately knew that it was Nicholas. It reminded me of the ordeal that lay ahead of me to save the hotel. I felt my stomach tighten in knots.

'Okay. Enough of this; I have work to do,' I turned away to check my email.

Blast! everything was up to date. I looked at the antique cuckoo clock on the wall behind the reception. Four o'clock. Time was dragging. I checked my lipstick in the mirror. It was fine. I looked over and caught Ken staring at me. I stared back and we found ourselves locked into a new game, a staring game. A tall, Asian man in his thirties entered the lobby and broke our intense concentration.

His posture was somewhat stiff as he positioned himself in the centre of the lobby like a statue and looked around. Something about him was most definitely off.

As I stepped out from behind the reception desk to greet him, he surveyed me coldly from head to toe, which didn't take long as I'm only five feet and six inches tall. He then gazed assessingly at Ken.

'Can I help you?' I asked.

'No. I'm fine, thank you,' he replied tersely. Ken and I watched in fascination as he sat in each of the lobby armchairs in turn and then returned to stand in the centre of the room and looked around again.

'Are you a guest here, sir?' Ken asked, knowing full well he was not.

'No,' he replied. Ken and I exchanged glances. I broke into a cold sweat and my mind went into overdrive. What if he were a hotel inspector? Or one of those mystery shoppers? Or one of those sanctimonious busy bodies just waiting to find fault, like the lack of wheelchair access, and threaten to go to the media or the hoteliers' association? No, he was a scout for a Hollywood producer, looking for a location. Wait, no, what if he were a suicide bomber? I was on the verge of freaking out when Loretta appeared beside me and joined our surveillance. I quickly brought her up to speed on the alien form who was now incomprehensibly running his finger around the shelves and book cases.

'What's he doing now?' she whispered.

'He's not baking a cake, that's for sure,' said Ken.

'I'll ask him,' said Loretta and strode over to him determinedly.

'Good afternoon, sir. May I be of assistance?'

He looked annoyed by her interruption. 'Dust. You have dust.' he accused and held up his index finger.

'Yes. It's a natural design feature,' Loretta replied, at which point Ken and I almost cracked up.

'Amusing . . . but I can assure you this is a serious matter,' he turned to me. 'Are you in charge here?'

I panicked for a moment. 'Yes. I am the general manager.'

'I have questions.'

'Ask away.'

'My boss wishes to stay here, and I always pre-inspect the hotels she stays at.'

'I see. And you are?'

'Tony. Personal assistant to Ms Ivy lee.'

'I see, Tony. And is Ms Lee anyone we should know?' I noticed Loretta frantically waving me over. 'Please excuse me for a moment.'

I hurried over to the reception desk. 'What's up?'

'Ivy Lee. She's the biggest Instagram influencer in Asia,' whispered Loretta.

'Never heard of her,' I shrugged.

'Hello!? She runs a fashion blog. She's like mega,' Ken interjected.

'Okay. So, she's kind of important then.' Was I missing something?

'If she likes the hotel, that could be big for us, right? Solve all our problems, duh!' Loretta pointed out.

'Oh! I get it now!' Was I really so out of touch with the world? The implications of the impending visit dawned on me. I took a deep breath and returned to Tony. He was frantically messaging on his phone.

'Hello, again,' I greeted him, smiling obsequiously. 'I apologize for making you wait. Please, allow me to show you one of our best rooms?' he slowly raised his eyes from his phone.

'No need,' he said abruptly. He held up his phone to me with a nasty smirk.

'I think you should check your social media. Specifically, follow Ms Lee.'

Ken and Loretta looked at me, concern writ large on both their faces.

'Check out Ivy Lee, would you Ken? Like now would be good,' I said, half in panic.

'On it.' Ken started to tap energetically on his phone. 'Oh God, this is bad. Very bad. Very, very bad!' Ken groaned after a few moments.

'Tell me,' I prompted, dreading what he would say next. Loretta snatched Ken's phone and looked at the screen.

'Well?'

Loretta looked ashen. 'Let's just say that Ms Ivy Lee's Instagram and Twitter accounts are on fire. And when I say "on fire" it's like a nuclear bomb has just been dropped.'

Tony interrupted us at that moment, 'She doesn't like dust. She'd absolutely freak out if she caught a glimpse of those disgusting old chairs!'

I needed to act fast and somehow fix this. I was in such a flap that I didn't even have time to panic.

My mouth didn't wait for my brain to engage, 'Well, dust is an inevitable part of life. Even the Ritz has its own special brand of dust. To expect no dust would be an impossible ask. You will note the floor upon which you stand is as spick and span as any room in a private hospital. Cleaner even, I should say. And the crisp, white Egyptian linen in our rooms has a higher thread-count than even the Savoy in London. It's a shame you didn't inspect the superior suite I was about to offer Ms Lee, at 40 per cent discount.'

I even surprised myself with that torrent of bullshit, but I was gratified to note that Tony's jaw had dropped. 'As for those "disgusting old chairs",' I continued, now in full spate, 'they were a gift from our very own prime minister, Mr Yew, to Mr Chan. They are French eighteenth century. In fashion terms, vintage, and vintage is all the rage now. But then, Ms Lee would, I'm sure, know that.' God, sometimes I amazed myself with what emerged from my mouth. Even Ken and Loretta looked like they had been turned to stone, their eyes as wide as saucers.

Tony started to pace around the lobby muttering to himself like a roomba that had bumped into an immovable object and couldn't get past it. He approached me hesitantly.

'Well . . . I—' he began.

'Can I help you with anything else, Tony?' I asked. 'No? I suggest you take yourself home.' I ushered him out like an unwanted cockroach. It took but a few seconds for Ken and Loretta to join me at the door, their faces frozen in shock.

'You go, girl! That was amazing,' Loretta beamed at me.

'Thanks. But it won't fix the damage which that flea of a man has caused.'

'Maybe not,' Ken had a look on his face which meant he had had a brainwave, although he kind of looked like he needed to go to the toilet.

'Well, out with it!' Loretta snapped.

'I have this friend, Sheila Tay. She's also a fashion blogger.'

'Oh, so you want her to bring us down too?' Loretta jumped the gun.

'Do you want to hear my idea or not?' Ken folded his arms and glared at her.

'Carry on, Ken. Thank you,' I nudged Loretta.

'Well, Sheila has been looking for an opening to take down Ms Lee from her perch for ages. Says Lee's views on fashion has become bias as to the extent of free products she is given. She's not focused on what people see as art or progressive creativity.'

Loretta and I stared blankly at Ken.

'So?' Loretta prompted him.

'Really? So obvious.'

'Not to us, obviously,' Loretta rolled her eyes. I elbowed Loretta again, this time harder.

'I'll get Sheila to post a challenge against Lee's review of our hotel. One virus kills another?' Ken seemed extremely pleased with himself. His constipated look had transformed into a smile.

'Okay. Saying what exactly?' I asked. Fashion was not my forte.

'Well, that's the hard part. You need to come up with a pithy retort, just like you did to that slug Tony earlier.' Ken started to type.

'What are you doing, Ken?' Loretta peered over his shoulder at his phone screen.

'I'm getting Sheila primed.'

'What?' Feeling a sudden panic attack, I lunged for the tourist brochures.

'Clara. Focus.' Loretta grabbed my hands. 'Close your eyes and imagine I'm Tony.' Her voice was calm and measured.

'Okay. I . . . I—' My heart rate had accelerated phenomenally. 'I can't think of anything. I really can't.'

'Okay, Shelia is in. She will post when we are ready,' said Ken. Not that it helped the situation.

'Yeah. You're right, Clara. You just don't have it in you,' Loretta whispered nastily in my ear. I couldn't believe it. She was my friend and not meant to make me feel worse. 'The dust in here is terrible,' she hissed having transmogrified into Tony. What emerged from my mouth next was certainly not directed at Loretta.

'Look, you weasel of a man, this hotel is beyond the vanilla, brainless, fashion blurb Ms Lee churns out, like cheap, knock-off jeans in China, which, by the way, are more outdated than those eighteenth-century chairs in the lobby. This hotel has heritage and classical history infused with modern ideals that provides its guests with the comforts of home and the luxuries of their dreams. So, there!' I opened my eyes and saw Ken furiously typing. 'Oh, my God. You didn't just . . .'

He had. He had taken down my rant, word for word, and had pinged it across to Sheila.

I'm not sure if I fainted or just phased out, but for a few seconds the world went blank. And then I found myself seated in the office, Loretta and Ken staring intently at me.

'What happened?' I asked.

'Will you or shall I?' Loretta said to Ken.

Ken explained it like this: Sheila Tay, who admittedly wasn't as well known as Ivy Lee, simply posted her own review of the Duxton which, as it transpired, was a glowing five stars, ten out of ten. It turned out that she herself had stayed here less than three weeks ago with her boyfriend, and people felt her humble but honest review was genuine. Or, maybe it was the fact that she had first Instagrammed her post to her sister, Charlotte Tay (recently engaged to venture capitalist, John Chu) in China; Charlotte had called her best friend, Eileen Ma (Peter Ma, the property billionaire's youngest daughter) in Singapore and had breathlessly filled her in; Eileen had texted thirty of her friends, including Emma Kwek (granddaughter of Robert 'Palm Oil King' Kwek) in Malaysia, whose cousin, Jane Kwek, had gone to Oxford and was friends with the Yew family, who owned half of Singapore's commercial real estate, shopping malls to you and me.

Sheila then simply *had* to message her friend Kim Wei (the Instant Noodle heiress) in Singapore and Justina Khoo, whose family owned one of Singapore's biggest banks. Finally, it had reached Clare Leong, the daughter of Michael Leong, the owner of the fashion 21 empire in Singapore, Hong Kong and China.

All of them also posted to their Facebook, Instagram and Twitter pages.

Let's just say that, by the end of the day, Ms Ivy Lee and her errand boy, Tony, were old news and Sheila was the new reigning queen of the blogs. Her Instagram following had grown by several thousand. And, *alamak*! this was the big news of the day.

In the two days that followed, bookings at the Duxton had gone up by 60 per cent. Our little stunt had paid off. But social media attention is notoriously short-lived and interest soon palled.

My focus returned to Nicholas, whom I still needed to track down. I had no choice but find him and throw myself at his mercy. The hotel's future depended on it.

Chapter 5

At 6.30 p.m., two days after my run in with Ms Ivy Lee's errand boy, Tony, my left knee began jiggling. I was seated at a long table, with Ken and Loretta, in a side room beside the noisy kitchen, which seemed to be perpetually redolent with the smell of boiled cabbage. Which was odd as we never had cabbage on the menu. A chicken-stock soup, followed by a seafood stir fry was being served along with a mountain of fluffy, white rice. I wasn't really all that hungry, so I stood up to pace back and forth like one of those poor, demented tigers in a cage at the zoo.

Ken and Loretta began to eat hungrily, eyeing my hyperactive perambulations with misgivings.

'So, what am I to do?' I asked.

Having finished her soup, Loretta wiped the corner of her mouth with a napkin, 'Do? About what?' Clearly oblivious to the torments preying on my mind.

'Mr Chan. He wants me to convince Nicholas Tate to help us save the hotel, because he's apparently some kind of a marketing genius,' I summarized my quandary as succinctly as I could, before subsiding into my chair. I reached for my rubber band. I had lost count of how many times I had replaced it. I twanged away.

'Really? You mean blue-blazer guy?' Loretta paused in her assault on the seafood stir.

'You mean the guy you insulted?' Ken butted in.

'Yes, him, Ken. Thank you,' I said repressively and spooned soup into my mouth. My stomach had gone from not being hungry to gurgling like a blocked drain now. 'So, now you can understand my dilemma.' I twanged my rubber band in a bid to break my worrying stream of thought.

'Well, you are the GM now, so you . . .' Loretta made a forward motion.

'So I . . . what?' I had no idea what she meant by her gesture.

'So, you call him up and ask for a meeting,' Loretta rolled her eyes.

'Yes, I could do that. But that won't work, will it?' I buried my face in my hands to obliterate the sense of hopelessness.

'Why not? No phone-card?' I could hear Ken laugh. This didn't help and I glowered at him.

Loretta nudged him in the ribs. Surely he could see that I was clearly not in the mood for jokes. I gathered myself together, drawing in a couple of deep, fortifying breaths.

'He's working for our competitor, so how can I ask him to help us? But Mr Chan expects results.'

Loretta placed a stilling hand on my hand as she saw that I was teetering on the brink of another twanging episode.

'Well, one step at a time, okay? You don't know until you try.' She held my arm in a strong, comforting grip.

'Do it now. Call him,' Ken exclaimed with barely supressed excitement in his voice.

My soup swirled in my bowl and I watched it go round and round with a sense of detachment.

'Clara.' My name was being spoken. 'Clara!' This time a little louder and I was shaken by the arm. I snapped to attention although it took me a moment to collect my thoughts.

'Where did you go, girl?' Loretta asked worriedly, seeing that I had indeed phased out.

'Sorry, I was miles away.'

'You sure you're okay?' Loretta asked worriedly.

'I'm good.' Ken had told me to call Nicholas, that much I remembered.

'D'you have his number?' asked Loretta.

'No, but Google will have his office number.' I quickly consulted Google on my phone and found the number. I hesitated only for a moment before calling.

A female voice answered and, after much back and forth, and being put on hold thrice, I finally established that Nicholas was out for a meeting with a client. I also discovered that he frequented a popular café on Saturday mornings and that I could try and reach him there.

As I hung up the phone, Ken and Loretta asked in perfect unison, 'Well?'

I started inhaling deeply. 'He's not returning to the office today, but he'll be at a café called Forty Hands in the morning.'

Loretta and Ken gave each other high fives, but missed each other's hands.

'Wait. You guys surely don't expect me to go there?'

'Why not? You have to,' Ken shrugged.

'What would I say to him? I haven't seen him since that terrible evening when he was here in the hotel, and I was . . . well . . . not very nice to him.' I could feel myself flushing.

'We just need a foolproof plan. Now listen,' Loretta took charge, 'sit down and listen.' We did as we were instructed. 'You just need to go to the café, act as if you go there all the time, and act surprised when you bump into him.' Loretta seemed to have it all worked out.

'And then I just ask him for help?' I couldn't believe that it would be that simple.

'Child's play,' said Ken. Not that it helped.

'More like mission impossible.' I buried my head in my folded arms on the table just as Barry, one of the hotel butlers, entered with a bottle of champagne in an ice-bucket and three glass flutes.

'Compliments of Mr Chan on your promotion,' he announced and deposited his burden on our table. We exchanged glances.

'Well, don't just sit there, Ken,' said Loretta, 'open it.' She gave me a great big bear hug, so tight, I almost passed wind. Ken popped the cork on the bottle, distributed the flutes and poured us each a glass. The three of us raised a toast.

'To tomorrow. May you bring him over to our side—and win his heart as well,' Loretta winked as she clinked glasses with me.

'Cheers. But I'm not really—'

'Hush,' Ken interrupted. 'You're going and that's that.'

I sipped the champagne still distrait. What if Nicholas refused to listen to me or help us? What then?

Chapter 6

Having tossed and turned all night, breaking at least three rubber bands and almost calling off my mission twice, I walked through the front door of the Forty Hands café—and bumped into a blonde woman with a beehive hairdo.

I couldn't help but notice that she was in skin-tight, black leggings, that almost looked sprayed on, together with a bright orange t-shirt. I noticed these things because it was about as far north of what I was wearing as to be ridiculous. As for me, I was in a yellow summer dress with brown Doc Martens nine holes. I felt conspicuous because everyone else seemed to be in active wear. Had I inadvertently walked into a fitness centre rather than a café?

Undeterred, I stood at the counter and awaited my turn. Unfortunately, despite my determination and brief surge of self-control, it wasn't long before I began tapping my foot impatiently and twanging the rubber band. The café was getting busier and the last thing I needed when I confronted Nicholas was an audience. My mouth went dry at the thought.

Kyle, the young barista was taking his sweet time with my order, carefully measuring out the ground, Ethiopian beans, which the café prominently proclaimed on prodigious posters, and placing it to percolate in the coffee machine for the perfect brew. I silently thanked him for his dedication to the art of producing an immaculate cup of coffee but wished that he would hurry up.

As the queue stretched even further behind me, I could see that my café latte had almost reached its zen point as the hot milk was poured in, uniting the yin and yang elements for the classic cup of coffee. The crowning glory was a floral pattern in the foam that was added with a few subtle twists of a skilled hand and, voilà!

By this time, however, I didn't mind the wait—in fact, I needed Kyle to dilly-dally and allow me time to brace myself for my forthcoming ordeal.

'D'you want me to add a little something to make it extra special?' he asked.

'What did you have in mind?' I asked, momentarily distracted.

'A touch of sweetness perhaps?' Kyle reached for a bottle of caramel syrup. By now, I think I would have agreed to just about anything, even if it had been tomato ketchup. My hands were shaking so much that, were I to hold the coffee, I just might've turned it into a smoothie.

'Yes, yes, give me a shot of that.' It would certainly give me a sugar high and help to perhaps steel myself to make what I was about to do look like an accident.

I took deep breaths and told myself, you can do this, Clara Tan, so, woman up!

With the coffee in a very shaky hand, I managed to find a vacant seat. It was a seat without a packet of tissues to stake a claim to it. I took a sip of the latte. It was everything I had expected. Sweet, aromatic and tasty. Time to check my phone.

LORETTA: IS HE THERE? HAVE YOU ASKED HIM YET? PLEASE
        TELL ME HE'S THERE AND YOU'VE ASKED HIM.

MR CHAN: CLARA, WHAT NEWS?

I placed my phone face down on the table. I wasn't ready for this inquisition. Did they think this was going to be easy?

The place was filling up and not with just the gym fanatics whom I had first noticed. Even this early, and on a Saturday, the little café was packed. All around me were crisply dressed teenagers who looked like they had just materialized from a TikTok video or some online, millennial-fashion site where people, who are clearly too old for the clothes, shop.

Laptop users nursed the coffee they had bought over an hour ago; a tribe of yummy mummies with perfect, doll-like kids; a random guy who thought wearing sunglasses and a cap indoors made him look cool.

I realized that I had chosen a seat from where I could see everyone who entered and exited the café.

I couldn't see Nicholas yet. I wondered whether he would arrive on his own or have a bunch of children nipping at his heels. A thought flashed through my mind—why would it matter if he was married or had kids? I could still ask for his help.

But . . . who was I kidding? Of course I hoped he was single and that he would still remember me. Chemistry is a strange thing, don't you find? It just melts the brain and we fall in love.

But, chemistry aside, would he recall how rude I had been to him the last time around and just ignore me today? Although, if I were being honest with myself, he didn't just tick some boxes—I genuinely found him attractive, which was making me all the more nervous. Why? because I knew that my approach to finding someone I liked was to imagine the life I might have together with them. The problem was I never actually spoke to them openly about what I wanted. That perhaps explained why I was still single. I didn't open up to them and as such never connected with them at the right level. That, and the fact that I was already on autopilot, rearranging the paper napkins in their holder. I must have already done and redone it a dozen or so times since sitting down. I had been so engrossed that I missed seeing Nicholas enter the café and sit down at a table off to my right. I just happened to look in that direction and there he was.

I tried to compose myself by straightening the cutlery by my cup a few times, not even sure when and how a fork and spoon had ended up on my table. I aligned them anyway. I could see that Nicholas was poring over a book, *How to sell Anything to Anybody!*

by Joe Girard, which was ironic because we wanted him to help sell the Duxton as a hotel of choice.

I knew what I needed to do, so, without further ado, I approached him circumspectly like a predator creeping up on its prey. Three. Two. One. I counted down my footsteps in my head. I studied him for a moment longer. Up close, he was even cuter than I remembered.

Stop it, Clara, I chided myself, *I was a woman on a mission and this was so not the time for a fantasy-man hunt.* My plan was to bump into his chair and spill my latte and then make some lame excuse, simultaneously pretending to be shocked to see him again. I say 'my plan' but it was actually a cunning scheme hatched by Loretta in collaboration with Ken.

Here we go. I held out my coffee. My mouth was now so dry that my tongue cleaved to my palate.

Come on Clara, do it, NOW!

Just then Nicholas laughed out loud at something he'd just read . . . and I sailed right past him.

Damn it. I couldn't do it. Now what?

I was so angry with myself I could've screamed. I had allowed myself to fantasize about my meeting the man of my dreams for the second time. Not that the first encounter had ended well, I reminded myself. But this time, I would lock eyes and just like in a movie and, in that very instant, we'd both know that we were destined to spend the rest of our lives together.

However, right now, holding the half-consumed latte with a Ferrari-red-lipstick smear on the rim of the cup, it felt as far from the silver screen as it was possible to get. I had to get a grip.

My anxiety shifted into overdrive and a cold sweat beaded my brow. My immediate reaction was to twang my rubber band, which I did far too energetically with my free hand, causing it to snap, and fly off, only to land in some poor guy's oatmeal.

Now what was I going to do? Not about the oatmeal, my rubber band. I needed something to twang. Taking the scenic route within the café, looking for a rubber band, I returned to my table. Having also failed in my mission to find my rubber band, I subsided in my chair.

Sitting next to me now was a man and his young daughter. The girl was about six or seven years old, I assumed. She was colouring in a book with some pencils.

I hesitated for a moment, but then my compulsion got the better of me, so I leaned over and arranged her pencils in a neat row, apologizing sheepishly, 'Sorry, OCD.'

The man with her, who I assumed was her father, just looked at me and smiled.

Another man joined our table. A spindly guy with a head of thick, spiky, black hair which stuck straight up in the air. He unfolded a newspaper haphazardly and started to read. I could feel my hands twitching with an urge to reach over and straighten the pages of his newspaper.

I inhaled deeply, but then I just snapped. I reached over and straightened the pages for him. Not that the response I received was in any way grateful.

He gaped incredulously at me and made a big show of retrieving his paper, loudly clicking his tongue all the while, causing the people around us to stare.

I pretended that I had no idea what his problem was and pulled out my phone. My finger hovered over the keypad and then I began to type.

CLARA: I COULDN'T DO IT. SORRY. I JUST FREAKED OUT.

Within seconds.

LORETTA: TAKE A DEEP BREATH. IS HE STILL THERE?

CLARA: YES.

LORETTA: BE YOURSELF. YOU CAN DO THIS, GIRL.

I pondered on her reply for a moment. She was right. I had to be myself. I knew the hotel's future pivoted on my success with Nicholas today. But I could not deny that a part of me wanted to do this for myself. I felt something for Nicholas. I knew it was crazy—I barely knew the guy. But oh, how I wanted us to hit it off. None of this hostility and awkwardness. Besides, Loretta was always right. I could do this, or rather, I had to. I had dawdled long enough.

My introspection was broken by the man with the newspaper. He seemed to be mocking me with his eyes. I tried to ignore him. But then, as if to push a button, he leaned forward and flapped the pages of his newspaper in my face.

I could feel my blood pressure rising and my hands tingling with the urge to grab the newspaper and straighten out the pages again. He did it again.

One of my hands jerked out spontaneously, but he drew the newspaper out of my reach as if he were enjoying tantalizing me. He then crackled the pages again.

A trigger had been activated, a red mist descended and clouded my sense of reason. My lungs filled with air.

'I have OCD, you jerk! Not funny.' Before the last word had tumbled out, I was the cynosure of all eyes. The entire café had fallen silent. It was too much. I felt myself trying to twang the rubber band that wasn't there. I had no choice but get out of there, pronto.

I shot to my feet, turned on my heel and made for the door. This time, I took the shorter route, which meant I'd have to squeeze past the table of perfectly turned-out mothers and their babies. My plan was derailed by two, neatly dressed, wide-eyed children who now blocked my path, one blonde and the other Asian with straight dark hair, both looking like they had answered a casting call for 'children who could haunt your nightmares'.

'Sorry, I need to get past. Thank you. If you could just . . .' I whispered. The two devil children remained glued to the spot. I turned to the mothers, 'Could I get past, please?'

Stern faces bore down on me, deprecating my gall to have even made such a request.

'Please move,' I pleaded again quietly, deeply embarrassed by the fact that everyone was looking at me as if I were a freak. Two of the mothers false smiled at me as if to say the kids would stay exactly where they were. I flicked a desperate glance towards Nicholas to check whether he had left. And if he hadn't, to ascertain he wasn't laughing at my predicament. But he wasn't there. He had gone. It was like a rock had just hit me in the stomach. Another cold sweat blanketed my body. One of the mothers—blonde, in skinny jeans and box-fresh, expensive heels—leaned away from her conversation with her friend to appraise me.

'Something we can do for you?' The tone was more sarcastic than an offer.

I felt my cheeks burn crimson. 'Everything is fine, thank you! I just need to get past and get some fresh air.' More people at the nearby tables were starting to turn around to see what was going on. I could see a woman with a ponytail and way too much make-up, in aerobic sports apparel that was way too tight for her body shape, shaking her head.

'Our children make their own decisions. Joy, Peaches, what do you want to do?'

I swear my jaw dropped as both children looked up at me and linked hands defiantly, effectively forming a barricade. They were clearly not going to move. My entire body started to itch and flush with blotches. My anxiety levels had catapulted to warp speed. It was the scenario of my nightmares. Normally I could control it by extracting myself from this type of situation. If it happened at work, I had no issues dealing with a difficult guest. But trapped by kids, whose mothers had ganged up on me like a cackle of slavering hyenas, was a bit much.

The little Asian girl, Joy, goggled at me, 'Mummy, she looks like a beetroot!'

Highly pleased with her little angel, 'That's a clever simile, Joy. No, the lady is just a tad embarrassed!'

'I'm scared,' whined Peaches. Now all four mothers were looking at me with forced smiles. I wished I could muster up the nerve to tell them that they were successfully raising their hell-born brats to become other children's traumatizing high-school experiences.

The next five seconds happened in jerky slow-motion like my life had been paused in a bad video.

Five. Nicholas magically appeared beside me, looking casual and handsome in a blue t-shirt and shorts. His muscular physique was now obvious. The four mothers' eyes snapped to him as if George Clooney himself had stepped up.

Four. At the last possible moment, I looked up straight into his eyes.

Three. I automatically smiled shyly. I could see that his eyes were filled with strength and he smiled back.

Two. It was as if Nicholas had witnessed everything, even the man with the newspaper. He just looked at the four mothers with steely-eyed derision.

One. Nicholas placed an arm around me, pressing me against his body before he spoke. Everything then sped up and returned into sharp focus.

'Hello ladies, have you met my friend?' he nodded towards me. 'She has been nothing but polite to you, but these two little children I can see are mirror-images of their parents, which if you bothered to examine closely, you may see a reflection you don't like.' Nicholas then knelt to be at eye level with the two kids, 'I think I know your fathers.'

Those were the magic words. Both Joy and Peaches broke ranks to cower behind their mothers and were no longer an issue. As were the mothers who just sat there, slack jawed.

Nicholas calmly escorted me to his table. 'You okay, Clara?'

'Yes. Thank you,' I breathed and unthinkingly picked up Nicholas's coffee and took a big gulp. 'Oops, sorry. I needed that.'

'That's fine.' With a gentle finger, he wiped away the foam from my upper lip. 'That's better. You look less like a rabid dog now.'

'Sorry . . .' I began again.

'Would you please stop apologizing?'

'Sor—' I almost said it again and then pursed my lips.

'So, what brings you here? Are you a regular?' I think Nicholas already knew that I wasn't, so I refrained from lying.

'No. I came here to see you actually. I've been trying to pluck up the courage to come over and talk to you.' My phone buzzed into life at that moment, but I ignored it.

'I see,' Nicholas replied.

'I—I've thought of you often. I hoped we'd bump into each other again,' I said hesitantly, beginning to relax again.

'That's nice to know. But how did you know I would be here?' Nicholas asked. I realized that I had walked into this one. Time to confess all.

'Okay. I did some research. I called your office last night and said I needed to talk to you about some urgent business. The lady who answered the phone told me that you were out for meetings all week, but that I might find you here on a weekend. So, here I am.' I looked away, deeply embarrassed to have ambushed him. Oh God, was I turning into a crazed stalker?

'You should have just asked for my phone number,' Nicholas stated the obvious.

'Yes, perhaps I should have.' I suddenly felt like an idiot.

'So, what was so urgent?' his eyes were now smiling.

I swallowed. 'I need some help. I thought it would be better to ask in person.' I hoped my eyes were also smiling now.

'Go on, I'm listening.'

'Oh, all right, then. It's like this,' I aligned my thoughts into a neatly organized speech, but then ended up just blurting out the words haphazardly. 'You're very talented, Nicholas. I know this because you've been working on a campaign for a major hotel chain. They're Duxton's competitors. Mr Chan needs your help to take his hotel chain to the next level, to protect his franchise. If not, we are doomed.' I looked down at my fingers, which were now tightly intertwined.

Nicholas remained silent for a moment. Then stood up. 'I'll be right back.'

I watched as he headed off towards the counter and place an order. He returned a few minutes later. 'More coffee needed, I think,' he said jovially.

I nodded.

'Now, firstly I can't disclose anything about the account I'm working on. It would be unethical. Secondly, how did you know what I was doing?' For the first time today, he looked serious.

'Oh, Mr Chan called a meeting and told us. He mentioned your name specifically. He has connections, I guess. That's all I know.' I could see his pupils dilating.

'I see,' Nicholas paused. 'Then, why is he not sat here himself asking for help, followed by getting out his wallet?' Nicholas leaned forward to emphasize the question. 'I mean, he can afford all the help he needs, right?'

'Well, actually I was just appointed the GM of the hotel. So, he sent me instead.' I then said something really stupid, 'I think he knows that I . . . well . . . that I maybe . . . sort of . . . like you.' Wrong thing to have said. It drew an immediate reaction.

'So, he thinks that can be used to get me to help you?' Nicholas was now being direct.

'No, it's not like that,' I denied this hypothesis.

'Isn't it? Look, I must go. Things to do, places to be,' Nicholas stood up as if to leave.

'Wait!' A sudden surge of courage erupted out of nowhere. 'Yes, you are right. But, in truth, I'm here as much for me as I am for Mr Chan. I wanted to see you, Nicholas.' My cheeks flushed red again. Nicholas looked consideringly at me for a long moment and then sat back down as the two coffees he had ordered arrived.

'Can you help at all?' I reached for his hand but accidentally knocked over one of the cups, spilling the coffee.

'Sorry,' I muttered, red in the face. 'I'll get some napkins.' I hurried back to the table where I had been seated earlier. Both the dad and the daughter still had their heads down, reading, the only two people in the whole café who were oblivious to my earlier debacle. Some fresh napkins were at the edge of the table closest to them, the ones I had rearranged earlier. As I took them, the daughter looked up with a smile. I glanced at the man with the newspaper. I rudely stuck out my tongue at him. Childish, I grant you, but it made me feel so good. The little girl mimicked me. The man shrank back behind his newspaper. Returning to Nicholas, I sat down and mopped the spilled coffee. He gallantly took some of the tissues and wiped the table. I waited for him to say something. But he just sat back, looking at me enigmatically.

'So,' I broke the silence, 'can you help?' His eyes were just locked on me. 'Please say something,' I was now tired of this waiting game. He then offered me his coffee. Fortunate as I had spilled mine.

'I'm prepared to help you,' he said finally, 'but only after I've completed my work for the other client. I should be done in about a month or so. Would that be okay?'

I sighed, 'Not really; it may be too late by then. We hear they're moving against our franchise aggressively. Some campaign called "Renaissance".' Something I said struck a nerve.

'How do you know about "Renaissance"?'

'I have my sources too.'

'I came up with that name myself. It's my take over plan.' Nicholas seemed rather proud of the fact that his campaign was the talk of the town now. But it was also zeroed in like a missile at my employer.

I fidgeted in my seat. 'But that means you are coming after us,' I protested. I needed to know his intentions and I was also feeling defeated and deflated.

'I'm not; my client is. But haven't you forgotten something?' Nicholas asked. I looked at him puzzled. 'The other reason you claimed to be here . . . or doesn't that matter anymore?'

The penny suddenly dropped. 'Yes, of course it does.' I realized my second chance was now presenting itself but was also about to slip away. I changed tack.

'Let's have dinner. Tonight?' I was amazed at my boldness. While waiting for his reply, I was already thinking ahead about where? I would make a suggestion to show him I was independent. The hotel, of course, for dinner. It would be perfect. Chef would cook up a storm and it could be on the house. That was decided then. Well, almost, I still hadn't received his reply. What if he refused? What then. I would have to think of a plan B.

'Clara,' he said dryly.

'Yes?'

'I'd love to.' Did I just hear him accept? Oh wow! 'Anywhere you have in mind?' he asked.

'Yes, actually, the Duxton, at eight tonight,' I said confidently. 'Fine.'

My phone buzzed again. 'I need to run. Sorry.'

'Going anywhere fun?'

'Kick-boxing class.'

He grinned. 'Now that I would like to see.'

Without thinking, I said, 'You can come with me if you like.' I regretted it almost immediately.

'Sure, why not?' Not the reply I was expecting. He stood up.

'One second,' I fired off a text on my phone.

CLARA: MISSION ACCOMPLISHED. GET CHEF TO PREPARE A NICE DINNER FOR TWO AT EIGHT.

A few seconds later.

LORETTA: BRILLIANT! YOU GO, GIRL. I'LL TAKE CARE OF THINGS AT THIS END.

'Okay,' I said to Nicholas, 'I'm ready.'

And with that I stood up as well and headed for the door. An idea struck me then like a bolt from the blue. Some inner demon thirsted for a teensy-weeny bit of revenge. I stopped by the table of the four yummy mummies.

'Give me a second, Nicholas.' I drew a deep breath and grinned like the proverbial Cheshire cat. Turning to the yummy mummies, I said, 'I'm Clara.' I extended my hand to the lady with the ponytail and skin-tight active wear. It took her a few seconds, but then she reluctantly shook my hand as if it were a slice of wet fish.

'I'm the general manager at the Duxton Hotel. Should you and your friends ever wish to pop in for afternoon tea, on the house of course, I look forward to making you feel as welcome as you made me feel.' I then bowed to her and her cronies and withdrew.

'It rather seems that justice has been served, ladies,' said Nicholas. He then looked at me, his green eyes kindling with something akin to amusement.

'Really?' I laughed.

Chapter 7

Why, you may ask, would I invite a man I hardly knew, but felt a deep romantic connection with, to be potentially beaten to a pulp in a boxing gym? Well, why not? He had volunteered to come with me of his own volition . . . so that meant he knew exactly what he was getting himself into, right? And, well . . . I would like to think he wouldn't have invited himself along if . . . you know . . . he wasn't interested in me, too. At least, I hoped so. Although he may not have specifically expected this—if you'll allow me to explain:

My uncle, Chin Wei, says that the smell of a boxing gym, or any gym, for that matter, that considers itself a real, old-world gym with sawdust and spit, is historically not a pleasant one. He once described the bouquet to me as a cocktail of stale sweat infused with the aroma of a fisherman's tackle box. Yuck!

Thanks to him, it was how I now described it to others. Well, except to Nicholas. Perhaps an oversight on my part.

Anyway, to add some perspective, we were not referring to the minimalistic, concrete box kind of gym with a row of high-tech treadmills, neither were we describing a gym with a sit-up bench that never got used other than to tie one's shoelaces on. And we weren't talking about a gym with a colourful array of massive, rubber balls on which only a trained seal could balance—God forbid, no.

Those places were not gyms anyway, but health clubs for those with broad-shouldered credit cards or corporate memberships. Perhaps, worst of all, they were places for bored, narrow-minded housewives or yummy mummies like the ones I met at the Forty Hands Café, who spent their time gossiping and looking disdainfully at us normal people, instead of working out their oversized egos.

No, none of that was here. The gym into which Nicholas had now stepped into was about as raw as any gym you could imagine, and he stood gaping opened-mouthed at the threshold. The paint on the walls was flaking and the whole place was stained with sweat, spit and blood spatter, so much so that it ought to have carried a health-hazard warning. My uncle felt that a fresh coat of paint would destroy its patina of history because his father and his grandfather had founded the club back when rickshaws trundled along the filthy, rat-infested streets and fighters didn't wear padded, leather gloves. He claimed that the walls spoke their own language.

'I'll get changed and meet you over there by the ring.' I pointed to an elevated ring in the centre of the open space. Its floor was a large square of stained canvas stretched over flexible wooden boards and fenced in with two rows of inch-thick rope. It was old school, and I could tell from Nicholas's pale face that he was already beginning to feel sick.

'Okay,' he replied numbly. I walked away to the changing room. I could see the club members eyeing Nicholas. They were a ragtag mix of men and women in faded old singlets and baggy shorts, which was the standard attire for this place. They had all stopped their workouts and were whispering in groups to each other. It was as if an alien had beamed down from the mothership.

Reeling from this assault on his senses, Nick spoke, 'Good afternoon, everyone. I'm Nick.' He was greeted by silence. It was a hostile environment which discouraged the ingress of rank outsiders and foreigners. I decided that he would survive the five minutes it would take me to change behind the old curtain that provided the most rudimentary of changing-room facilities.

'Put these on,' I heard the voice of my uncle command.

'I'm sorry, what?' I heard Nicholas reply. I could imagine him looking at the stocky figure of my uncle, who had a missing front tooth, cauliflower ears, a vicious-looking scar across his right cheek and an overall visage that resembled an old, leather, boxing glove. The scar was the result of an accident when he had worked in the docks and not, as one would automatically assume, the outcome of a knife fight. But I think he rather revelled in the minatory mien it lent to his appearance.

I wished I could have been the proverbial fly on the wall just to see Nicholas's face at that moment.

'Put on,' my uncle repeated. I pictured Nicholas trying to decipher my uncle's fluent Singlish. Now the old man would be handing him an armful of stinking and highly suspect leg, arm and body protectors. I knew the drill by heart.

'Umm,' was all Nicholas replied. At this point I had to laugh. 'I can hear you, Clara,' he growled as I emerged from behind the curtain. I couldn't help but laugh again as I climbed into the ring. 'Look,' he said, 'perhaps this wasn't such a good idea.'

'Nonsense,' I said bracingly. Nicholas looked around with misgiving at the people staring at him.

'I don't exactly feel welcome here, Clara.'

I glared at the other gym members, 'What? Never seen an *ang mo* before? He's with me.'

The effect was immediate and they all went back to their workouts like a switch had been thrown. Out of the corner of my eye I could see my uncle glowering at them which was probably what had defused the tension rather than my snarling.

'What exactly is an "ang mo"?' asked Nicholas.

'A redhead.'

'What?'

'It means a redhead.'

I shuffled my feet in front of him, in the universal invitation to fight.

'I'd do as she asks if I were you,' advised my uncle. I'm not sure what it is but, as soon as I step into the ring, I transform into this whole other person.

Nicholas donned the protective pads albeit wincing and moaning a bit. It took him a while to figure out which pad went where, and my uncle had to assist him. After what seemed like an eternity, Nicholas looked like an apprehensive, martial arts, tackle dummy.

'Ready?' I asked.

'I think so.' My first kick was to his right shin-guard and he buckled like a sapling in a cyclone. I hadn't even put that much power behind it.

'Christ!' he muttered as he staggered back to his feet. I squared up to him again and delivered another swift kick, this time in the centre of his stomach pad. Perhaps this one had a little too much power behind it because it sent him rocketing backwards against the ropes.

'Good God!' he spluttered.

'You all right?'

'I think so.' My favourite move came next: a rear-swinging back kick. The only problem was that it struck Nicholas when his guard was down and caught him on the chest knocking him flat on his back.

'Come on. Block me!' I spat.

'Wait. Hang on for just a moment,' Nicholas inhaled deep gulps of air. 'I have no idea what—'

I was so in the zone, I delivered a punch to his head guard that effectively killed his sentence.

'No time for talking,' I said, stupidly thinking he was okay and enjoying our sparring. I circled him like a tiger about to pounce.

'Stop!' he clumsily clambered out of the ring.

'What's wrong?' I peered over the ropes.

'Look, I only came here out of curiosity to see what you did here; not to be made a fool out of in front of these . . .' he broke off, 'people and have you kick the shit out of me.' He ripped off the protective pads one by one and flung them to the ground. I could see that he was upset and angry. My adrenaline levels were so high that I had completely overlooked the fact that he had never done this before.

'Sorry, I thought you might enjoy it,' I said with all sincerity.

He glared at me, his green eyes glittering with rage. 'Enjoy it? Do I look like I'm a sadomasochist?'

'Chill, Nicholas. It's not like you're hurt. It was just some fun,' I strived for nonchalance as I climbed down to join him.

'Look, this was a mistake,' he stalked out through the door.

'Nicholas!' I called out. But he had gone. I realized that I had made a huge mistake. I should have sensed that he was not okay. But then, he was a guy; don't all guys know how to take a punch or a kick? Was he that delicate?

I shook my head and hurried off to the shower room. Cold, rust-coloured water emerged from the faucet. The plumbing in this building was a bit eccentric, a lot like my uncle, and we were always nagging him to fix it. I splashed cold water on my face. *God*, I thought, *what have I done!*

I had blown it again with a guy. What was wrong with me? I always managed to mess things up. Clara: the disaster zone. Was I beyond hope? Was I fated to end up a spinster? A gentle tap on my shoulder turned me around.

'Come on, I'll get one of the lads to spar with you,' my uncle gestured to me to get back in the ring. I couldn't help but smile. Perhaps he was right. I should go a few rounds to work off my stress. He could always tell when I was anxious.

I just had to hope that Nicholas was okay and that he would forgive me eventually.

Chapter 8

I always take a siesta when I get back home after a workout and sleep like the dead for an hour or two. I did the same today. When I woke up, I still had a earpiece in one ear. The wires were tangled around my neck and an empty packet of cheese-and-onion crisps lay next to me on the pillow. I had allowed myself a treat, having burned some calories. My mouth tasted sour and I felt, to be honest, a bit sweaty and gross. Darkness had taken over from daylight and was creeping in through the curtains. But wait!

Something had awoken me, and it hadn't been my alarm clock. What was I not remembering? You know the feeling, when you wake up and think what the hell was I meant to be doing right now but, for the life of you, you couldn't remember? Well, that was how I felt right then.

'Shit!' I remembered. It hit me like a smack in the face. I was meant to be having dinner with Nicholas. I looked at the clock on my bedside cabinet, 6 p.m. I had to get my skates on.

As I scrambled to shower and get ready, I couldn't help but recall the last time I had seen Nicholas. There was a strong chance he wouldn't even show for dinner. Why would he? I sat on the bed, hair dripping from the shower. Perhaps he had calmed down enough to realize that he had overreacted?

Then again, it was partly my fault. Poor Nicholas was most probably not expecting to be pounded to a pulp in a kick-boxing gym, and would, I am sure, have much rather preferred to have spent his afternoon in a comfortable chair, sipping coffee.

I suddenly felt more optimistic and dried my hair. The evening would be perfect, I thought, and he would show up. I kept the positive thoughts coming and imagined him looking suave and smiling. The perfect image to have in my head as I applied my Ferrari-red lipstick. I could hear my mum banging around in the kitchen.

'Mum, I won't be needing dinner,' I hollered, hopping around in one shoe.

'Mum,' I called again. But I wasn't really expecting a reply, knowing full well that she would be in the thick of preparing a stir fry. I squeezed my foot into the other shoe and, headed for the door, simultaneously summoning a Grab taxi with a swipe of my finger.

'Love you, Mum,' I called out. A moment later, my mother appeared at the kitchen door. A sweet smile broke across her face,

'I'll give your dinner to Mr Lee next door.' She then vanished just as suddenly into the nether regions of her kitchen.

My optimism started to wane as I sat in the rear of the taxi looking out the window. Nicholas wouldn't show and I would be sat there in the restaurant, alone and ignominious. Stood up like some sad old spinster. I went to twang my rubber band, which was absent. I twanged away anyway. Nothing I could do now; I was on my way and would just have to see how the evening panned out.

As I stepped nervously into the restaurant, I immediately saw the table for two, set to perfection with silverware, a starched, white-linen tablecloth, complete with candles and two empty chairs. I looked at my phone; it was 8.15 p.m. Here I was, standing in front of a table which was set for a romantic dinner, and I was alone. The dark forebodings I had had in the taxi had crystallized. Nicholas was a no-show; I could feel it.

Well done, Clara, you did it again, I thought. *Botched another chance to get to know Nicholas better.*

Ken and Loretta appeared from the inner sanctum of the kitchen, both beaming widely.

'Why the long face?' asked Loretta. Ken lit the two candles on the table and their flames exuded a translucent, almost magical, glow over the table. It looked so perfect.

'Thank you so much, both of you,' I faked a smile, conscience-stricken at the amount of effort they had put in.

'We made it real nice and Chef has prepared a roast duck,' Ken announced excitedly. My stomach knotted up. It was time to confess to both of them about the fiasco that had transpired.

'I'm not sure he's coming,' I bit my tongue guiltily. 'Sorry.'

'What are you talking about, girl?' Loretta looked perplexed.

'Well . . . I . . . kinda upset him,' I muttered.

'You did, but let's move past that. You look lovely, by the way.' Those words and that voice almost made me faint as my brain plunged into denial of some sort.

It was Nicholas. He was standing right behind me. 'Sorry, I didn't mean to keep you waiting.' He drew out a chair for me.

'Thank you,' I said lamely. What else could I say? I was in shock.

'Come on, Ken. Let's leave these two alone,' Loretta gave me a conspiratorial wink as she hauled Ken away.

Turning back to Nicholas, I was silent for a moment. My hand reached for his and I whispered, 'I thought you wouldn't come.'

'I almost didn't, but we Tates never stand up a dinner date.' He grinned and clasped my hand warmly.

'I'm very glad about that,' I said, smiling now. 'I'm sorry about the gym.' It needed to be said.

'It's okay, but I'm not sure I'll join you again.' We both laughed at that, just as the duck arrived.

'I hope you like it. This is a speciality here.' I inhaled the aroma.

'I'm sure I will. It looks wonderful.'

Dinner went off without a hitch. We tucked in and stripped the delicious meat from the bone. Egg noodles were served alongside some healthy greens. Everything seemed perfect. And then the topic of the hotel came up to kill the moment.

'Do you serve western cuisine as an alternative?' he asked, wiping his mouth with the corner of a napkin.

'Why?' I asked. 'Was something wrong with the food?'

'No, it was good. But if you're serious about taking on the competition, this place needs to broaden its appeal.'

I looked at him in dismay. My hands had already begun to straighten the silverware. Until then I hadn't felt any symptoms of my weird compulsions.

'The hotel was renovated not long ago actually,' I said.

'Yes. But polishing an antique vase isn't all that is relevant at this juncture,' he said.

I reflected on his words for a moment. 'People like charm,' I offered.

He leaned back in his chair. 'People want charm, yes, but they also want fusion. Old meets new, the cuisine of today, that is; not something I can get in Chinatown from any market stall.'

At this point, I swear my brain abruptly disengaged and my mouth dribbled out words I wish I had had time to reconsider before giving them utterance. 'That's unfair! The chef here is highly regarded. In fact, that is an insulting thing to say.'

I waited for him to challenge me again. The spoons were now being aligned to form a perfect square along with the knife and fork. His hand came down on mine to halt my fidgets.

'Look, Clara,' he said calmly, 'you asked for my help, but you won't accept my input. All I'm saying is that this place needs to offer modern fare with tinges of the traditional. People want to eat something wow! not something good. It's seeing what you have through a fresh, new lens.' He leaned in and took my hand in his warm clasp and smiled.

I could feel my emotions clouding with anxiety. 'I asked you here so that we could show you what we offer, but you have insulted my hotel.' He released my hand and sat back in his chair. An awkward silence ensued.

'This is pointless,' he declared as he stood up. 'You don't need my help. I wish you luck and thank you for dinner.'

I remained glued to my chair for a good fifteen minutes, I think, just staring at the empty plates before Loretta eventually came in. Her inner radar had already detected the evening had been a disaster. She put her arm around my shoulder in a gentle embrace.

'Plenty more fish, dear,' was all she said, with a reassuring smile. She was right. Why should it matter? I invited him over for the sake of the hotel. I barely knew Nicholas, anyway. Perhaps he wasn't the man for me after all. But . . . I really thought we were hitting it off. I had hoped that the second time around we would have bonded better—but he had walked off again.

Chapter 9

Two weeks had passed since the disastrous dinner with Nicholas. I was at the front desk, thinking about him. I wondered what he was doing. I wondered if he was okay. I wondered, as a man, similar in stature to Nicholas, just walked past me and exited via the main doors, what he was wearing. A blue shirt? Men tended to have a certain day on which they wore a certain colour shirt, don't they? At least that's what I had noticed on the way to work, most days: Mondays, was white; Tuesdays, pin stripes; Wednesdays, pink; Thursdays, blue and Fridays was dress down, so a polo shirt. Yes, it was a blue-shirt Thursday for Nick, I was sure of it.

People all around me were going about their business—coming and going, visiting friends, or attending meetings and above all, eating. The thing is, any time is eating time in Singapore, so everywhere you go you will find a food market of some kind. I suddenly felt acute pangs of hunger and could almost smell the aroma of the delicious, hot-and-spicy, local dishes wafting in through the lobby to tantalize my taste buds.

I imagined Nicholas in his office, lounging in his office chair with his feet up on his desk and staring at the ceiling, pondering some theory. He seemed to have opinions about everything, and

I was sure he would ponder the theory of life. Or maybe the theory of relationships.

His theory would be that hating someone felt disconcertingly the same as loving the person. He would run through the gamut of reasons that caused him to believe in this hypothesis. Love and hate are visceral, he would conclude, because of which one's stomach knotted and twisted at the mere thought of a person; that the heart would pound with such violence that it could almost be visible through your clothes. Thoughts of that person deprived one of sleep and appetite for food. Even the very thought of eating would make the mouth go dry and trigger nausea. Any interaction with the person in question would spike the blood pressure to levels so far above the norm as to make the eyeballs bulge. The body and mind would barely be under one's control, scaring one to death. You would then realize that love and hate were two sides of the same coin. Whichever side one was on, one of the feelings would eventually triumph. The heart and the ego would be at war. Yes, this was his theory.

Or perhaps it was mine.

No, he would have read a book that had expatiated that most men are driven by ego and that most women are ruled by the heart. His own ego would be screaming like a fire-station siren for him to walk away from having any further contact with me. He would realize that we were from very different worlds and had nothing in common upon which to build a relationship. He would think of me as someone who liked to beat the living shit out of things as a hobby, whereas he himself liked to chill and listen to classical music.

He would have noticed my condition. Sure, he could empathize, but would it mean that he would have to resign himself to spending a lifetime ensuring that he didn't inadvertently leave his socks and underwear strewn around the bedroom floor for fear of giving me an anxiety attack?

My thoughts were now wholly consumed with what he would be thinking. I needed to rationalize this and process it in my head. I needed to make sense of my ridiculous obsession with him.

He was a man I barely knew, and each time I had met him, I somehow managed to make a mull of the moment.

I took a deep breath as an explanation of sorts dawned on me. In the movies, there's this thing called the 'meet-cute' which, in essence, is that moment when the romantic couple meet for the first time. It's supposed to be amazing, amusing or ironic and even charming. I had felt all, not merely some, of those feelings when I had first met Nicholas on the steps of the Duxton Hotel. Okay, perhaps it had not been as scripted or romantic as depicted in the movies where the sassy, ball-busting female character mistakes the handsome new lawyer for the janitor; or where the impossibly cute secretary rear-ends the Porsche of the guy who turns out to be her new boss. So, what had gone so horribly wrong? I pondered further.

But wait! What about true love? Wouldn't that relegate nonsensical notions of a meet-cute to mere fantasy and entirely contrived. And here's what you don't learn from romance movies: in real life, the meet-cute wasn't the least bit cute. It was more like a meet-awkward and sometimes even a meet-kill-me-now encounter. Which was exactly how my first encounter with Nicholas had ended. It was all beginning to make sense now.

And another thing they don't tell you in the movies: it takes a hell of a lot longer than that split-second moment in a movie scene to know that this person is something other than just a momentary blip on your radar.

I tried to summarize my thoughts into a simple conclusion: the meet-cute was this big, fat delusion created by the fantasyland of Hollywood and nothing more. That meant I was thinking way too much about having met Nicholas and what it meant to me.

Oh my God! After that brain melt, I needed a break, so I grabbed my handbag and headed for the door. Some fresh air would help bring me back to earth. As I hit the pavement outside the hotel, my mind was still buzzing. Yes, my feelings for Nicholas weren't real. Except sometimes . . . sometimes, the meet-cute could be real. I felt confused again as the voices of fantasy and reality continued their debate inside my head.

Strangely enough, on my last birthday, my mother had prophesied that I wouldn't really know myself until I turned thirty. I knew that the smell of roses nauseated me. I knew I didn't like classical music or old movies and that being on a boat made me seasick. Oh, and above all I hated being late for anything. I also knew that it was probably some sort of cosmic coincidence that on the first day of a new job, one would invariably sleep through the alarm, misplace the mobile phone and the subway would naturally be running way behind schedule. Why was that?

I stopped for a moment and looked at my reflection in a shop window. I was missing out on seeing Nicholas on a pale-blue-shirt Thursday. It was the colour of a clear sky beneath which dreams came true.

My thoughts drifted again to the dinner fiasco and hoped that he had walked home that day with a face contorted with deep remorse. I had hoped that he would call me and apologize. But then again, why would he?

Perhaps I ought to have called him. Perhaps I was wrong. Perhaps his comments were true, and we did indeed need to look to the future. And . . . perhaps I needed to do the same too instead of trying to start something with Nicholas.

I continued my walk, inhaling deeply and just allowing myself, for once, to think about nothing at all.

Chapter 10

I lay on my side, my cheek pressed into my pillow. He was braced against me, pressed against my back, warm as toast. His voice was a hot whisper in my ear as he ground himself against my butt, 'I'm going to turn you over.'

I was now lying prone on my stomach. I could feel his weight on me, pushing me down into the mattress. I tried to push back against him, using my elbows for leverage, but he whispered to me to lie still and crawled over my back, his knees straddling my hips. His fingertips feathered along the sides of my breasts. His warm breath on my neck made the small hairs on my nape stand up. I couldn't get a decent lungful of air. He was too heavy and I was too turned on. Sensitive, forgotten parts of me blazed into life. My anxiety vanished and I felt myself floating free of my earthly self. I clawed against the sheets.

The realization that I was having a dirty dream about Nicholas Tate suddenly stirred and I teetered on the edge of waking up, but I kept my eyes tightly shut. I needed to see how far my mind would take this. I felt myself being sucked back in.

'I'll do anything you want, Clara, but you'll have to ask me.' His voice was soft and lazy but firm. It was like he could see right into my soul, but I couldn't see his face.

Even though it could potentially shatter my flight of erotic fancy, I rolled over on to my back, the bedclothes twisting around me. I was caught up in a tangle of arms and legs, both his and mine. I realized I was turned on and wet as I gazed into his moss-green eyes. I gasped in pleasure. I was not afraid. Or sorry. I wanted him so much. There was so much delicious weight, pressing me down. Hips and hands. I moved against him sinuously, feeling him bite back a groan. And then I realized something shocking: I desperately wanted him inside me.

The thought was echoed by my words, true and undeniable. A butterfly kiss on the wild pulse in my jaw confirmed what I already knew. It was stronger than mere attraction; darker than mere wanting. It was a restlessness between us that had never had a true expression, until now. This explained everything. We wanted each other, but neither of us knew how to approach it, let alone confess to it.

The sheets were now sizzling against my skin. He was tied up in knots over me as well. I felt his hands slide feverishly over the curves of my body. I had never had anyone burn for me like this. I was shamefully turned on and even though I was underneath him, the look in his eyes confirmed that it was I who was winning this joust. I tried to tug him down to kiss me, but he evaded and tantalized.

'Clara,' he whispered, 'you know you've wanted this all along.' His radiant smile tipped me over the edge and I woke up. I jerked my hand away from my damp panties, my face crimson in the dark. I couldn't decide what to do. Finish the job, or take a cold shower? In the end, all I did was lie there.

I stared at the menacing silhouette of my hotel uniform draped over the foot of my bed until my breathing returned to normal. I looked at my digital clock. I had four hours to repress this memory.

It was 7.30 a.m. on a white-blouse day for me. My reflection in the mirror confirmed that my Burberry raincoat was longer than my uniform's skirt which my mum had managed to shrink in the wash, so I looked like a high-class call-girl, en route to a hotel penthouse, wearing only lingerie beneath the coat.

I jest, of course; I was wearing my staid uniform not to mention the very sensible underclothes. And yes, it was raining, albeit it was just a warm drizzle. I was not in the habit of wearing a raincoat in the tropics for no good reason. Although I just needed an excusé— any excuse—to wear the Burberry, considering that it still sat on my visa card, four months later.

I had to get the bus today, as I was on a shoestring budget, having frittered away way too much on Grab taxis and expensive raincoats.

I could barely climb from the kerb to the bottom step of the bus without flashing a fascinating glimpse of my underwear. As the doors swished closed behind me, I knew this skirt was a catastrophic lapse in judgment. I should have just thrown it away and worn another one. The enthusiastic honking from a passing car driver as I walked to the hotel confirmed this. If Robinsons had been open this early, I would have ducked in and bought myself a pair of trousers.

I could get through the day, I told myself bracingly, although I would need to remain seated for the entire day which, considering I spent most of the day stood behind the main reception desk, could be a challenge. I entered the lobby of the Duxton and, of course, Ken was at his desk. Why did he always have to be at work so early? Did he never go home? Did he sleep in the hotel?

I was hoping to have a minute or two alone to get settled in for a long day. But there he was. I hung up my raincoat and scurried for cover behind the reception desk. If I focused on the skirt as my main issue, I could ignore my flashbacks to last night's dream.

Ken raised his eyes from his work and stared at me for a moment. 'Your skirt, did it shrink in the wash?' he asked before abruptly turning back to the papers on his desk.

Just as I conjured up a suitably squelching response, a guest arrived and approached me. He looked like he was in his mid-thirties, six feet tall and Brad-Pitt handsome. The blue of his eyes was so vivid that I was drawn to them like the proverbial moth. He was looking at me like he was reading my mind. Oh, my goodness, did he look a bit like Nicholas or was my mind playing tricks on me?

'Isn't it cold in here?' he asked. I immediately thought of the air conditioning. Singapore, famously known as the air-conditioning nation, was paradise in the humid heat; but when it rained, everywhere indoors became freezing cold.

I returned my focus to the man before me. My mouth opened but no words emerged. He made a circular motion in front of my face as if to ask whether there was anyone home. 'Sorry. Zoned out for a moment. Yes, it is a bit chilly. Can I help you, sir?'

'Yes, I have a reservation under the name Jared Barnes.' He smiled.

I checked the system, confirmed his booking for three nights and checked him in. He asked to be shown to his room, which was a perfectly normal and reasonable request. Unfortunately today, in what amounted to a tennis player's headband as a skirt, and Ben the bell boy was nowhere to be seen, I felt anxious, knowing I would have to show him up myself.

'Ken,' I called out. But Ken was busy talking to a stout guest, and giving him complicated directions on a tourist map.

'I'll show you to your room, Mr Barnes. It seems our porter is busy elsewhere.' I announced and set off towards the elevator. I could feel his eyes boring into my back. I twanged my rubber band a few times as we entered the elevator and the doors closed.

I could feel the friction of the tiny panties on my thighs as I shifted uncomfortably and discreetly tried to pull down my skirt. I was pretty much wearing a swimsuit. I was so embarrassed.

I watched him eyeball me, his eyes dropping to the floor to my shoes and then rising up again. Did he just check me out? He did; I swear he did.

He looked young, until he looked up and his eyes were a man's—speculative and hard. My ankles wobbled. I wore low, three-inch heels at work, nonetheless I felt like I was on stilts.

'So, what would you suggest as good sightseeing while I'm in town?' he asked. I smiled sweetly and rattled off a list of the local attractions.

He appeared to consider them for a moment and then clarified, 'I meant tonight; something fun, like a cool wine bar.'

I'm sure I blushed. 'Oh, Ken, our concierge, would be happy recommend a few places.'

Now why did I say that? He was obviously just making small talk. *Wake up, Clara!*

'Okay. I'll make a note to ask him.' The doors to the elevator opened and he gestured me out first. A gentleman perhaps, but it was more than likely that he wanted to watch me from behind as I walked down the hallway to his room. I showed him into room 204, explained where the safe, the mini bar and the TV remote were and prepared to leave.

To my surprise, he then hits me with a request I wasn't expecting. 'Would you like to join me for a drink later?' I whipped around in surprise.

'Before you say you can't fraternize with the guests, allow me to say, I do understand that rule. In any case, I will be standing outside at 9 p.m., at which time you finish your shift. It's a free world, Clara, and no one need know,' he smiled.

All I could do was smile lamely, 'Okay.'

The instant the door closed, I ran to the elevator, my mind awhirl. *What was I thinking . . . okay?* I was a mess but, on some level, it felt strangely good. It wasn't as if I was seeing anyone anyway. The voice of Loretta bounced around in my head now: 'Live a little,' she would often say.

And why the hell not? I would be fired if anyone found out; but who would find out? I would be seen; Singapore had eyes everywhere. I twanged my rubber band as I stepped into the elevator to go back down to the reception desk. Then it struck me: how on earth had he known that my shift ended at 9 p.m.? Perhaps he was a secret shopper deployed by Mr Chan. I had no idea what to do: ignore him or live a little. I had no choice; I would have to ask the one person I trusted the most, Loretta.

As I emerged from the elevator, Loretta arrived at work. She barely had time to place her handbag in the office before I collared her.

'Coffee. Now. Need a chat.' I hauled her off in the direction of the kitchen.

'What's up?' she yanked me to a standstill.

'He's-so-handsome asked me out. What do I do?'

Loretta cast her gaze heavenward in silent prayer before towing me into the staff room. With two steaming cups of the cheap in-house coffee, we parked ourselves in a corner.

'Now breathe. Who has asked you out? Nicholas?'

It was my turn to roll my eyes, 'No. The man in 204. He just checked in.' I was now pressing my knees together so hard that my knee bones ground against each other.

'A guest?' the tone of her query said it all.

'I know.'

She took a sip of the coffee, winced and then swallowed. 'Okay. You know you can't, right?'

I leaned forward and squeezed her wrist. 'I know. But you are always telling me to "live a little".'

Loretta squinted at me, surprised that I remembered her sophistry and wasn't sure whether I was being serious.

'I had a . . . dream . . .' I paused. 'A very dirty dream about him and then this guy shows up and . . .'

'You dreamt about this guy?' Loretta was clearly not keeping up.

'No. Nicholas.'

'Wait,' she palmed me to take a moment. 'You had a dirty dream about Nicholas. Was it good?'

I shook her arm. 'Yes. But forget that. Tell me what to do about this guy.'

She looked at me like I had broken out of an asylum. 'D'you know this guy?'

I let go of her arm. 'No. It was just a connection. Like he could read me. He asked me to meet him at 9 o'clock tonight.' It finally sank in.

'I see,' she said dryly. We headed back to the front desk. Just as we reached it, as if by magic, I saw him exit the elevator and cross the lobby floor towards the main entrance.

I tried to make eye contact but chickened out at the last minute and sauntered casually to my chair. I desperately wished I could casually saunter out of here and all the way home and change out of this skirt.

'Hey,' said Loretta sharply, 'was that him?'

I wondered whether I should confirm it or not. 'Who?' I asked evasively.

'D'you know him?' she repeated, only this time her tone had risen by an octave.

'Oh him,' I responded. 'Yes, that's him.' There I had said it.

Immediately Loretta gave me a congratulatory thumbs up. 'Well, if you decide not to meet him—'

Ken magically materialized beside us as he caught the tail end of the conversation.

'Meet whom?' Ken leaned across the desk.

'Never you mind . . . women's business,' I waved him away like a pesky fly.

'Describe this dream you had about Nicholas . . .' began Loretta. I didn't react. 'Your face has gone red . . . all the way down your neck.'

'Stop looking at me!'

'Can't. You're directly in my line of vision,' Loretta moved in even closer.

'Well, try,' I snapped.

'It's not often that we see such a provocative, thigh-revealing outfit in the workplace. In the HR manual for appropriate business attire, is it—' she wiggled her eyebrows.

'It shrank in the wash,' I tried to stretch it to a more workplace-acceptable length by tugging the hemline on either side.

'No wonder he wants a date,' Loretta winked lasciviously.

'So, who have you been seeing lately?' I abruptly changed the topic.

'David, his name is David and I'm seeing him this evening.' She beamed at me like the proverbial cat that had swallowed the proverbial canary. 'It's a shame you don't have a date, otherwise we could have made it a double.'

I mulled over her words. It was exactly what the doctor ordered to get over Nicholas and forget all about Mr Barnes.

'I'll find one between now and the end of the workday,' I replied, determined to hire a guy if push came to shove or call a modelling agency and ask for the catch-of-the-day. He would pick me up in a limo in front of the hotel and Loretta would be left with egg on her face.

'What time is your date?' I asked.

'Eight.'

'Where?'

'Are you serious?'

'Why not? I need to have some fun,' my mouth responded before my brain engaged in gear.

'Okay. Meet us at Harry's in Clarke Quay when you finish here.'

'Great.'

'So, who are you bringing? Not room 204?' she asked with an evil smile.

'No, of course not. I know other people. I'm not that pathetic.' I moved away from the desk and went into the office.

The day passed by in a flash and before I knew it, it was home time. Who was I kidding? I had no one to ask out. No one to flirt with. No one who would be desperate enough to want to spend an evening with me. I had no date.

I then thought of Loretta meeting her new man. She would be flirtatious and fun. She would listen with rapt attention to his spiel. He would be utterly captivated by her banter, her confidence and her sexuality. She would give him her sexiest come-hither look, non-verbally communicating to him that she was his for the taking. . . provided he played his cards right. I envied her at times.

As I stepped outside, I inhaled deeply and then set off towards the bus stop.

And there he was, standing there like it had been ordained. His teeth seemed whiter than before. His face clear and fresh. He looked extremely handsome.

No, not Nicholas; Jared Barnes.

'Hi,' he said.

'Hello.'

'I'm meeting some friends for drinks at a sports bar nearby, and wondered—'

'I'm sorry, I can't drink with a guest.' Now why did I cut him off so sharply?

'Understood.'

I turned away to continue on my way when he spoke again, 'I'll walk with you, if you don't mind.'

'Sure,' I infused a languorous ennui in my voice so he couldn't tell I was panicking on the inside. I surreptitiously assessed his appearance, comparing him to Nicholas in my mind. I was fairly sure that Jared wouldn't leave me high and dry halfway through a heated argument. He seemed more mature and confident. Besides, I was getting along with him just fine and I thought I ought to see where this evening would take us.

'Look. Just one drink with you and I'll leave, I promise.' His smile drew me like a magnet would an iron filing. Before I knew it, I was considering it. *Was I mad? He's a guest, Clara,* I reminded myself again. But then, what harm could it possibly do? Was I not the general manager now? I was just Clara, a normal woman who had just finished work and surely, I was entitled to have some fun.

'Okay. Why not?' Too late to retract now. I was committed. He smiled his beautiful smile again.

'There's a good bar and restaurant around the corner, Jigger and Pony,' I suggested the place just so I could have control, or at least the illusion of control, over the evening.

'Sounds wonderful,' he beamed. 'I'll tell my friends that I have other plans for this evening. Shall we?' As we strolled side by side, he fired off a message to his friends. And then I realized something. Why wasn't I feeling anxious? I should've been twanging away by this time. Instead, I was actually feeling rather good. Like a carefree little girl on the inside. This was most odd.

We chatted easily and naturally and arrived at the jam-packed bar. The heat generated by the closely packed human bodies created a weather system all of its own inside the pub. Humidity was high in the crush of bodies, battling for the attention of the bartenders. Three barmen skilfully mixed cocktails with the flair and pizazz of stage magicians.

I looked on as Jared manfully shouldered through the crowd, ordered two dirty martinis and then turned to me.

'You okay?'

'Yes, good.' I had to shout to make myself heard. I felt his arm draw me close to his side, which I kind of liked. I felt secure and protected.

'So, do you like working at the hotel?'

'Yes, I love it,' I replied promptly. The hotel was my life. As the drinks arrived, a fleeting thought of Loretta flashed through my mind. I wondered whether she was having as much fun as I was right then. A bar stool next to me became vacant and I was swept on to it by an arm.

'There you go. Much better,' he stood sentinel beside me. I crossed my legs as elegantly as I could in my miniscule skirt and I noticed his eyes flash down, then back to my face.

'I'm feeling a bit exposed today,' I decided to take the bull by the horns and deal with the elephant in the room considering I had just caught him looking at my thighs.

'This is strictly between us, right?' he asked. I was apprehensive about what he was about to say next but, strangely enough, there were no alarm bells or sirens going off inside my head or any other signs of an imminent panic attack. 'I liked you the moment I met you, but . . .' he trailed off. I couldn't believe it.

'But what?' I prompted impatiently.

'I knew who you were . . . sort of.' I was sure that my face reflected my bewilderment.

'What does that even mean?' I asked.

He turned into me and took a sip of his cocktail. 'I know Nicholas Tate. He mentioned you.' I could feel my tongue cleave to my palate, depriving me of the power of speech. 'I'm his boss, you see, visiting from London.'

I heard his words like they were coming from afar; the world had stopped, frozen in time and space. 'Are you okay?' he placed a gentle hand on my arm. There was no choice now: the threshold had been breached; I reached for my rubber band and gave it a twang. I could see the genuine concern in his eyes.

'You're his boss?' was all I could muster.

'Yes. But look, that has nothing to do with why we are here. I fancy you, Clara, straight and simple.'

I took a large gulp—not a ladylike sip—of my dirty martini. *Get a grip, Clara*, I berated myself, before excusing myself and heading to the ladies' room. I fished out my lipstick, my mood matching the savage red which, according to my mum, was vicious and the colour of the devil's underpants. In light of the fact that I was here, having a drink with the boss of the man whom I had mistakenly assumed to be my Mr Right, but had proved, without a shadow of a doubt, that he wasn't, and now that his boss had just declared that he liked me, I desperately needed the psychological confidence-booster provided by this colour. Thanks to my trusty, Ferrari-red lipstick, I could magically transform from an essentially monochrome and uncomplicated individual with a medical condition into a flamboyant woman in technicolour.

I rejoined him at the bar some fifteen minutes later, expecting to find he had either left or was chatting up another woman. Surprisingly, he was stood exactly where I had left him, sipping his drink, alone. I deliberately shelved the fact that he was Nicholas's boss and we continued to drink, talk and, if I were honest, having fun. The evening was perfect. I found myself thinking that I didn't want it to end. It did, of course, five martinis and several hours later.

It was late, too late to go back home and disturb my mum, so I decided to sleep at the hotel, not in Jared's room of course. There were limits to how far even I could bend the rules despite my being the general manager. All I could think of, as I drifted off to sleep, was Jared. His room, number 204, was directly above the room that I was in. I could almost smell him. I had no idea whether I dreamed about him or not, but I did wake up with a beatific smile on my face.

I had housekeeping send up some fresh clothes and it thankfully included a skirt that fitted. A new day had begun.

'You look a bit hung over,' commented Loretta. She knew me too well.

'No, I'm fine,' I replied.

She leaned in to sniff me, 'I smell date.'

'No,' I lied.

'Who was he?' Good God, the woman was like a bloodhound.

'"Lived a little" just as you suggested.' I beamed at her and sashayed away towards the kitchen. She caught up with me. I could see realization dawn on her and she glazed over. She followed me to the counter and watched wordlessly as I made myself a strong cup of coffee and then trailed me into the admin office. I pulled up a chair and collapsed into it.

'So, how was your date?' I asked her, deflecting the conversation from myself.

'Good. The sex was amazing. I kicked him out at 7 a.m. this morning.' My pathetic attempt at deflection had seemingly failed when she challenged me: 'Now, you. Tell all?' She had turned from a bloodhound into the dog with the bone and showed no signs of letting go. I looked at her, bleary-eyed.

'It was okay. No sex. But good company.' It was the truth.

'Wow! Clara Tan had a date at last. After how many years?' I knew she was mocking me.

'That's right!' I felt rather chuffed with myself.

'Good for you,' she smiled.

'Now I think we should get back to work.' And with that, the subject was closed. What I hadn't told Loretta was that I had agreed to see him again this evening.

Chapter 11

Never in my life had I felt as terrible as I did when I woke up that morning. Never. Not even when I had the chickenpox when I was five.

All I could feel were the exploding sparks of pain as I tried to turn my head or open my eyes or move any part of my body. I tried to work out a few basics like:

Who was I?

What day was it?

Where was I meant to be at that moment?

I lay as still as I could for a while, panting with the exertion of just being alive. My face grew scarlet as I almost started to hyperventilate. I forced myself to calm down and breathe deeply, hoping that that would make me feel better.

In . . . out, in . . . out. In . . . out, in . . . out.

Okay . . . Clara.

That's right. I'm Clara Tan, aren't I?

In . . . out, in . . . out.

What else? You had dinner.

Yes, I had dinner somewhere last night.

In . . . out, in . . . out.

Pizza! I had pizza.

And who were you with, again?

In . . . out, in . . . Jared Barnes. Out.

Yes, I was with Jared Barnes.

Stupid. Yes, I had allowed myself to get caught up in the moment again.

What was I thinking, going out with a guy I barely even knew?

In . . . out.

My memory began to return in dribs and drabs. A twinge of guilt shot through me. But why? *I was worried that Nicholas would find out.* So what if he did? He didn't own me. We were not even dating. Why was I being like this? Why was I even having this conversation with myself?

A familiar wave of despair engulfed me and I closed my eyes, trying to calm the throbbing in my head. At the same time, I remembered more about last night and the details started to emerge.

I had gone back to Jared's room and stupidly helped him kill a bottle of single malt whisky. I never drink that much. Come to think of it, I never drink whisky. So, why did I agree to open it up—and why did we drink so much? It was certainly a few glasses more than we should have had. Which would possibly explain why I was feeling like death today.

Slowly I struggled to a sitting position and listened out for the familiar sounds of my mum in the kitchen; but I couldn't hear anything. Strange, I thought? It made me feel safe and secure, you see, when I could hear her pottering around the house. So not hearing her was mystifying, almost weird. In fact, it made me anxious. I then tried to rationalize it. The flat couldn't be empty because she never left home without telling me. Wait! A flash of memory then flew through my mind. She had told me something the other day. But what was it? I closed my eyes and thought hard. Something about . . . Yes. I remember now. She had started Tai Chi with a bunch of neighbours and would be at the beach. *How could I have forgotten that?*

The mounting anxiety and guilt gradually increased my heartrate like a drumbeat that summoned my emotions to battle.

But why? I had nothing to feel guilty about. I reminded myself again that I was not in a relationship with Nicholas. This was crazy. I needed to clear my head and get a grip. Why did he wield such power over me? I just couldn't explain it. Me, alone with my thoughts could have negative consequences, and therefore, I needed to hear my mother.

Clara, you can control this, I tell myself, which I often can. So why was I finding this so hard now? My head was still pounding and I felt shaky—but I had to get moving; distract myself somehow. I then remembered that it was an off-Saturday and I wasn't working that day. Perfect, I thought. I would go out for a cup of coffee, preferably somewhere quiet, and try to get my head together. No kick-boxing today. I managed to convince myself that it sounded like a plan.

I caught a glimpse of myself in the mirror and didn't like what I saw. My skin was a pasty green, my hair was in clumps and my mouth felt dry, but worst of all was the expression in my eyes: a blank, miserable self-loathing. Last night, I was given a chance—a fantastic opportunity on a silver platter to get to know someone cool and successful—and what did I do? As always, I tossed it in the bin—and hurt a nice and decent man. God, I was a disaster.

An hour later, after a few litres of water and a couple of Panadol, I made it to Orchard Road, to lose myself in its anonymity. As I walked on, the balmy air almost made it almost possible to forget about last night. Almost, but not quite.

I bought a bottle of water from a 7-Eleven and gulped down its entire contents in one go. I walked into Starbucks and ordered a large latte and tried to drink it like it was just a normal day and I was just another girl out on a Saturday for some weekend shopping. But I couldn't do it. I couldn't escape the relentless churn of thoughts inside my head, like a record on repeat, playing over and over and over.

Flashes of what happened last night started to piece together in my memory. The mists in my mind started to clear.

Nicholas . . . something about Nicholas. Then as if a magician's wand had been waved, memory returned. Oh God!

If only I hadn't mentioned Nicholas. If only I hadn't been so *stupid*.

It was going so well. He really liked me. We were holding hands on the sofa. He was planning to ask me out again. If only I could turn back time and replay the evening . . .

Don't think about it. Don't think about what could have been. It's too unbearable. If I had played it right, I would have probably been sitting here, drinking coffee with Jared, instead of alone. I would have probably been well on my way to starting a relationship with him. He had asked why I kept bringing up Nicholas.

Well, it was a fair question and wasn't it about time I was honest with myself as well as Jared?

The truth, Clara Tan, is that you like Nicholas and it's as simple as that. The way he talks, looks, drinks. Every cell of his being seems to stir something in you. Admit it and be done!

I was glad I had told Jared about how I felt about Nicholas. I had been honest and that was a value I held most dear. Jared seemed to respect that although I'm not sure why any man would want to hear about how I felt about another man? Stupid of me.

But, be proud, Clara Tan, you were open with him. Even if he did decide to walk away, I could only hope that we would remain friends. Miserably I took a sip of the coffee and a bite of the chocolate muffin. I was not really in the mood for chocolate, but I stuffed it into my mouth anyway.

The worst thing—the very worst thing of all—was that I was starting to quite like Jared. Was that real though? Or did I see Nicholas in him. They were similar in some ways, I guess. But Nicholas had something special, he seemed real. Jared seemed like he was just notching up conquests on some personal scoreboard.

Whoa, what was I doing? I was trying to find similarities in them.

Their looks were very different. Their smiles, their voices. What was I thinking? They were nothing alike. Except that they both were sweet and cute . . .

I was afraid that I was going to start blubbering at any minute, overwhelmed by the tumult of emotions. I brushed at my eyes roughly, drained my cup and stood up. Out on the street, I hesitated before setting off again, hoping that the breeze would blow away my stupid megrims.

My head ached, my eyes felt bloodshot and I felt I could really do with a drink or something. Just a little something to make me feel a bit better. A drink, or a cigarette, or . . .

I realized I was stood in front of Tangs, my favourite department store in the whole world. Five floors of clothing, accessories, furnishings, gifts and footwear. I had my credit card with me. I just needed a little something to cheer me up. A t-shirt or just a bubble bath? I *needed* to buy myself something. I won't spend much. I'll just go in, and . . .

I was already pushing through the doors. Oh God, just the ambience of the air-conditioning and the bright lights made me feel like I had stepped into Shangri-La. The make-up department was buzzing with the ladies having trials and getting their faces made up or testing perfumes.

This was where I belonged on a day like this. Except that, even as I was heading toward the t-shirts, I wasn't quite as happy as I expected be. I looked through the racks, trying to conjure up the excitement I usually felt at buying myself a little treat—but somehow, on this day, I still feel a bit empty. Nevertheless, I chose a cropped top with pink lettering on it that said LOVE. I tried it on, telling myself I felt better already. Then I espied a rack of dressing gowns. I could do with a new dressing gown, as a matter of fact. As I fingered a lovely, white, waffle bathrobe, I could hear a little voice inside my head—a censorious voice, like the one that chided me when I indulged in daydreaming vacuously about Jared and Nicholas. It was crackly, like a radio turned down low. *Don't do it. You don't need it. Don't buy it.*

But quite frankly, what did it matter now? It wasn't going to break the bank. I could afford it. Almost savagely, I yanked the dressing gown from the rack and draped it over my arm.

Then I reached for the matching waffle slippers. What would be the point in buying one without the other, right?

Then I saw the real prize—the array of shoes. High heels; they glittered tantalizingly under the spotlights. So many designs to choose from. I selected a pair of blood-red pumps, the exact shade of my lipstick, and squeezed a foot into one. God, it would kill me to walk in these but, oh, how sexy! I told the friendly looking assistant to find my size and, considering the price tag, she was back in a flash. $900, ouch!! Her commission for the day had been made.

The checkout point lay immediately to my left, but I ignored it. I was not done yet. I headed for the escalators and went up to the home-furnishing floor. Time for a new duvet set. White, to match my new dressing gown. And a pair of bolster cushions.

Every time I added something to my pile, I felt a little whoosh of pleasure, like a firecracker going off and for a fleeting moment, everything was A-okay. But, when the sparkling and iridescence faded and reality kicked in, I once again plunged into gloom and darkness. I looked around feverishly for something else. A huge, scented candle for Mum. A bottle of lavender-scented shower gel. A bag of handmade potpourri. As I added each item, I felt a whoosh— and then blackness. But the whooshes were getting shorter each time. Why wouldn't the pleasure stay? Why didn't I feel happier?

'Can I help you?' a voice cut into my introspection. A young assistant, in the Tangs uniform—a white shirt and black trousers— was eyeing my pile of stuff on the floor.

'Would you like me to hold some of these or get you a basket, while you continue shopping?' she wanted the commission. I looked down blankly at the stuff I had accumulated; it was quite a lot by now.

'No, don't worry. I'll just . . . I'll just pay for this lot.' Between the two of us, we somehow managed to lug all my shopping across the floor to the checkout point in the middle, and the cashier at the till began to scan the items through. The bolster cushions had been reduced, which I hadn't realized, and while she was checking the exact price, a queue began to form behind me.

'That'll be $1350.56,' she said eventually and smiled. 'How would you like to pay?'

'Erm . . . credit card,' I said and reached for my purse. As she swiped it through the card machine, I eyed my carrier bags with misgiving wondering how I was going to get all this stuff home.

Immediately my thoughts sheered away. I didn't want to think about home. I didn't want to think about Jared or Nicholas. Or any of it.

'Thank you,' said the cashier as she returned my card. 'Do visit us again.'

'Oh,' I whispered, flabbergasted by the size of the dent I had put in my bank balance. 'Yes, maybe when my credit card has recovered.' I tottered off to the exit before I was tempted to purchase something else I didn't need. I needed to sort myself out and get rid of these crazy impulsions. A brisk walk, albeit laden like a donkey with all my bags, and something to eat I decided. I was interrupted from these ruminations by my phone ringing.

'Hello.' It was Mr Chan. He wanted me to come into the hotel and his tone sounded urgent. I wondered what was wrong and, of course, agreed to come at once. My craving to binge shop was under control now but had been replaced by acute anxiety. Perhaps the hotel was going to have to shut down. It was Saturday after all and everyone was working but me. Perhaps I had been fired.

Oh, God, what could it be? I gave my rubber band a *twang*. The taxi journey to the Duxton took only fifteen minutes and I entered the lobby laden like a beast of burden with my shopping. Loretta rushed out to intercept me.

'They're all in the meeting room waiting for you,' her tone was excited and flustered.

'They?' I enquired.

'Just get in there, and I'll take care of these,' she quickly relieved me of my bags. I hurried away, even more anxious than I had been before.

At the threshold of the meeting room, my jaw dropped. Sitting opposite Mr Chan were the two people I never would have imagined to be there. My face must have drained of all colour because Mr Chan looked at me with concern.

'Are you all right, my dear?' he asked. I tried to find the words.

'Yes,' I lied and then subsided into the chair beside him.

'Hi,' Jared spoke first.

Then Nicholas, 'Hello Clara,' he smiled.

'Hello,' I replied to both, shooting a 'WTF' with my eyes. *Was I about to be fired?* I wondered. My head started to pound again.

Oh, God. Quick, think about something else. Look at the floor. Glance about the room. They were all looking at me now. As I caught Nicholas's eye, I smiled awkwardly. 'How are you?' I asked.

'Very well, thanks.' It was as if nothing had happened. He was either very cool or being extremely professional.

'Why am I here?' I twisted around to look at Mr Chan beside me.

'We have a situation, my dear,' he replied. This was it; I was done for. He knew about my assignations with Jared. Someone must have seen us.

'I'll resign,' I exclaimed.

Everybody exchanged puzzled glances. 'Why on earth would you do that?' Mr Chan asked. Oh, God, maybe he didn't know. What had I done?

'Look, Clara. Mr Chan has invited us in to help. The competitor has now announced plans to open a hotel just around the corner. Jared and I have been thinking. We like a challenge and feel we would like to help you instead. So, after much discussion, we have dropped the other account.' Nicholas looked at me enigmatically and then continued, 'So, no need to resign, Clara. We're here to help.' It was as if he understood my predicament and had just bailed me out.

'Yes. Nothing would please us more,' Jared added. 'In fact, I am so impressed with what I've heard about you from Nicholas that I agree one hundred per cent.'

'Really?' I wondered whether he was being sarcastic.

'Yes, my dear. So, I want you to now work with these fine gentlemen and come up with a plan. This is now your mission. It has been agreed that Loretta will take on some of your daily workload.'

'It will be a pleasure working with you, Clara.' Jared stood up and Nicholas followed suit.

'Likewise.'

'Right. Then I'll leave you to it,' Mr Chan patted me on the shoulder and left, leaving behind an awkward silence. Jared was the first to break it.

'Nicholas, would you give me a moment alone with Clara, please?' in a tone that brooked no argument. After a moment's hesitation, Nicholas nodded and left.

'Look, I—'

'No, Clara,' Jared interrupted me with a wave of his hand, 'it's all good. There's nothing to say. Nicholas is a lovely chap and I wish you both the best.'

'Thanks, but I—'

'All I ask is that it doesn't impact our work here. Which I know it won't,' he turned to the door.

'Wait!' I called after him. 'I'm sorry about last night. I wanted to be honest with you.' It looked like we would be working together, so I thought it would be professional to tread as lightly as I could over the ground that had turned into quicksand and to reconcile myself to keeping both these Englishmen at arm's length. Emotionally, that is. I then zoned back into the room as Jared started to say something.

'Well, we'll see you Monday then, bright and early. I've extended my stay here to focus on this account. Bye for now.' He semi-waved awkwardly and left.

Did any of that just happen? Was I dreaming? I shook my head and then followed Jared out.

'Clara, may I have a word, please?' said Nicholas heavily as I emerged through the door.

'Yes, of course.'

'I have no wish to make things difficult for you. I'm truly sorry for my part in this muddle. Perhaps we can be friends?' he held out a hand, which I immediately shook.

'Why would things be awkward?' I asked, which was silly really.

'Well, I know about Jared, your seeing him,' Nicholas almost blushed.

I stiffened at his words. 'Look, I like you very . . .' I broke off. I felt the familiar feelings threaten to engulf me, like I was about to buckle under his charm again, but I determinedly started again.

'I mean, why can't the two of you stop saying you know about the other and magnanimously wish me luck with the other. I'm not dating either of you, so why does it feel like I am?'

Oh, God, had I messed that up again? He looked at me like I had run mad.

'Yes. You are right, of course. See you on Monday, then.'

I watched him stalk off just as Loretta appeared. My heart thumped in panic. Nicholas must think I was bonkers.

'So, I hear you'll be working in collaboration with blue-blazer,' she winked.

'Working, yes,' I replied seriously as Loretta and I returned to the lobby. My stomach lurched as I knew it was going to be difficult to not fall in love with him again. 'I need to focus, Loretta. I can't allow my feelings to get in the way of my work. I was wrong to even think I could make it work with him.'

Loretta abruptly changed the subject. 'I like your new shoes by the way. I hope you don't mind that I snuck a peek.'

'Of course not. You can borrow them whenever you like. It's not like I will have a chance to wear them any time soon.' She leaned in and hugged me. 'Do you really like the shoes or was that just an excuse to change the topic?' I asked.

Her smile said it all. Tears sprang to my eyes. With her watching my back, how could I fail?

'So, where are you off too now?' she asked as I reached for my bags.

There was one place I could go. The one place I could always go. Home.

Chapter 12

On Monday morning I woke up early, feeling rather hollow inside. My gaze alighted on the accusatorial pile of unopened carrier bags in the corner of my room and guiltily flicked away. I knew I had spent way too much money on Saturday; I shouldn't have bought those shoes or that bathrobe and its matching slippers. But my mum loved the scented candle and shower gel that I gifted to her.

I had spent . . . I really didn't want to dwell on just how much I had spent. *Think about something else, Clara, and quick*, I adjured myself. *Something else. Anything'll do.*

Then I remembered the agenda for today.

I was acutely aware that, at the back of my mind, thumping quietly like a rhythmic beat on the bongos, were the twin horrors of panic and anxiety. I sensed their approach by the quickening of my heart rate, the pulsing of blood through my arteries and the cold sweat beading my brow. If I were to let my guard down, my neuroses would swoop in and take over my soul and I would be paralyzed by the fear.

I decided that if I simply ignored this vague foreboding, it would dissipate on its own and disappear. My mind would, today of all days, do as it was told. I would keep myself grounded and focused with the thoughts and activities that were important.

I got up, switched on the radio, took a shower and got dressed. The thumping was still there, somewhere in a crevice in my cerebrum, but gradually, very gradually, it was fading away and was barely discernible by the time I drifted into the kitchen to make myself a cup of coffee. A cautious relief flooded over me akin to the feeling when the painkiller kicks in and the headache recedes. I could relax at last. I was going to be all right.

My mum appeared like a ray of sunshine. 'Morning, dear,' she greeted me with the kind of smile that said no matter what I did or said, I was loved.

'Morning, Mum. Got to run, sorry. Love you,' I said, mechanically. Did I sound monotonous and shallow? On the way out, I paused to check my appearance in the hallway mirror. I looked okay. I grabbed my bag and set off.

Fresh coffee and a selection of biscuits were on the table by the time I arrived. The bus had been running late because a man's umbrella had got caught in the automatic doors and it had taken a while to extricate it. Not that it had been raining, but the mangled tangle of the umbrella had to be extracted by the irate driver and the doors put through their paces of health-and-safety checks.

Jared and Nicholas were already engrossed at the whiteboard, drawing complicated diagrams that the late Stephen Hawking would have been proud of. I knew what they were because I had seen them on a TV programme a long time ago. They were 'Mind Maps'. My mind could do with someone mapping, I thought, in light of the fact I struggled to understand my own emotions.

Jared spoke first, 'Okay. We think we have a nascent idea.' I smiled enthusiastically and he continued, 'We focus on the old-world charm of the Duxton Hotel but offer a series of rooms that are individually designed to appeal to multiple demographics. Everyone loves a cigar bar or a cocktail bar, so we add those in. That would also appeal to other people, both tourist and local, who were not staying at the Duxton per se. Maybe even a traditional barber shop.' He paused to see if I was following.

'With you so far,' I moved closer to the whiteboard, to indicate that I understood the mind maps. Which, of course, I didn't.

'This approach should work,' said Nicholas. 'The hotel has something that other hotels do not: the opportunity to be niche, boutique and different.'

'Exactly. We play to its strengths, but fine tune the services on offer to bring them into the twenty-first century,' Jared concluded the presentation. They were a duo act in full selling mode.

This, I knew, was about the time that I had to input something profound. I drew in a deep breath.

'So, basically, we already have the infrastructure but what we have is outdated, d'you agree? Take the bar, for example. A bar is a bar, but we need to make it a venue, a venue that draws in the crowd, not just guests looking for a nightcap.' I looked around for approval and Jared and Nicholas exchanged looks.

'Exactly, you've nailed it,' Jared high-fived Nicholas. 'A venue. I like that.'

I swelled with pride especially because that idea had just come out of nowhere. I was so pleased, in fact, that I helped myself to a shortbread biscuit.

Brushing the crumbs away, I asked, 'So how do we proceed? It all sounds so positive, but how would the wheels be actually put in motion?'

'We need a plan,' said Jared, 'as we already have the strategy. So, I'll work on a refurbishment budget and Nicholas here will work with you on a marketing plan.'

I wasn't sure what happened next. Perhaps an adrenaline rush produced by just looking at Nicholas had ignited a surge of creativity in me, or I had merely tapped into a mine of hidden talent deep within me. My next words caused the dynamic duo to go catatonic.

'How about, we rebrand the hotel, the "Duxton Heritage"?' I suggested.

Come on, say something, I thought into the deafening silence that ensued.

'That's brilliant,' Jared spoke first. 'You should come and work for us.' He then laughed. I assumed this was because what I had said seemed so obvious, rather than ludicrous.

'I have to agree. That's pure gold,' said Nicholas. 'The DUXTON HERITAGE,' he repeated in awed tones.

'Just perfect,' Jared concluded by a simulated punch of triumph into the air.

'Right. Then we go with that,' Nicholas clapped enthusiastically.

'I'm glad you like it,' I said, shyly. I refrained from any extravagant physical gestures and felt my modest verbal expression of gratitude would suffice.

'Like it? It could take us weeks to come up with stuff like that and you just snapped it out of thin air,' Nicholas exclaimed. His tone reflected his surprise, but he was smiling.

'So, I assume you will halve your invoice to Mr Chan because of my invaluable input?' I asked cheekily. From the sudden mood drop, I figured that this comment was less impressive.

'Ha! Maybe we could tune it a bit, but let's not get too carried away. We should take this to the next level,' Jared back-pedalled hurriedly, which was kind of comical.

I think my half-stifled giggle gave me away. 'Relax,' I said, 'I'm joking.'

'Yes, yes, very funny,' Jared replied drily and then took a gulp of his hot coffee.

'Clara,' said Nicholas, 'I'll shoot back to the office now and think of a plan. It may even be worth us researching a few competitors to see what works.' I loved seeing him smile. It made me come over all warm and fuzzy inside.

'Great,' I agreed.

'Cool. Maybe we can meet up later to see where we're at?'

Now why did he have to say that? I was screaming, *yes, I love you too*, on the inside.

'Good idea. I'll get to work unearthing an interior designer and producing a pitch for Mr Chan.' I saw them look at each other blankly and realized they hadn't thought this far ahead yet.

'Actually, I may know of a designer. So, leave that one with me. okay?' Nicholas said.

'Okay.' I agreed. 'So,' I asked, slowing down, 'when should we aim to update him?'

'Err. Today is Monday, aim for Thursday,' said Jared, packing up his laptop before heading for the door.

'Okay,' said Nicholas, 'I'll set up the required meetings with the designer and Mr Chan.' He stopped at the door and turned around, 'I'll see you back here at seven, Clara. Bye.'

'Why?' I looked up surprised.

'I thought we could brainstorm some design ideas?'

An imp of mischief derived a dark pleasure by making him wait for my reply, 'Okay sure.' He hurried off after Jared.

As I sat there alone, I couldn't help but wonder why they got paid the mega bucks if all they did was state the obvious and wait for someone else to come up with the really innovative ideas. But I guess the obvious was, sometimes, not quite so obvious when not all of us thought of it.

Chapter 13

It was 7 p.m. on Monday evening by the time Nicholas had returned to the hotel to meet with me. Loretta, Ken and I were halfway through a nice bottle of Australian red. Ken swore that it would help with the flow of creative juices. Not that I felt any different, to be honest, other than, after just a few sips, my face glowed a brighter shade of red than my lipstick. I decided to park my rule of not drinking on a work night because it had been a stressful few days.

'Run that by me again, would you?' said Loretta.

'Run what?' Nicholas asked.

'Listen, my boy, and you just might find out,' said Loretta bossily.

Nicholas obediently sat down, crossed his legs and looked expectantly at us.

'Okay, here goes,' I said, 'Eclectic and elegant is how this boutique hotel in the historical and storied neighbourhood of Duxton Hill can be described. Now part of the Duxton Heritage Reserve Collection of Hotels, the hotel makes a bold statement in hues of black, gold and yellow, with design elements borrowed from Chinese, Malay and European cultures. No two rooms are the same, so guests are in for an exclusive experience in any of its thirty-seven rooms. Foodies are spoilt for choice. They can enjoy local fare in the nearby Maxwell Food Centre, dine at the many restaurants and bars along Duxton Hill, or simply pop over to the hotel's modern Chinese restaurant, the Sanctuary.' I paused at this point and looked at Nicholas to gauge his reaction.

'Well . . . thoughts?' Ken prompted Nicholas, barely thirty seconds after my pitch.

'I . . . well . . . I . . .' It was the first time that I had seen Nicholas at a loss for words which, when I thought about it, was a worry. I had to say something.

'Oh dear. Was it that bad?' I asked nervously.

'No, not at all. Brilliant, in fact,' he said, his face reflecting his surprise and appreciation.

'Yaay!' Ken leaped out of his seat and offered Nicholas a high five which was disdainfully rebuffed, leaving Ken feeling very silly.

'Really?' I asked, wondering if I had heard right.

'Yes, really. I'm very proud of you.' I felt myself go scarlet with pleasure.

Having recovered from the rejected high-five, Ken uncorked a second bottle of wine and poured out a fresh glass of wine for everyone.

'Cheers, everyone,' Nicholas raised his glass. 'To Clara,' he added. We clinked glasses.

'Well, now that that's over, I think we need to be getting off, don't we, Ken?' Loretta's pointed message didn't get through, but an elbow in his ribs and a glare from Loretta drove the point home.

'Oh, yes. Must be off!' he declared.

'Are you sure? We can open another bottle, if you like?' I mentally kicked myself even before the words were out. Thankfully Ken had already chugged down his glass at one go, as had Loretta. The pair of them were red faced as they winked at me and staggered out. I couldn't help laughing.

'Clara,' said Nicholas.

'Nicholas,' I smiled.

'I managed to get an interior designer. I'm meeting her tomorrow if you'd like to come along. She comes highly recommended. She worked on the Raffles Hotel last year.'

'Sounds wonderful,' I heard myself say, not really paying attention to his words. The chemistry that drew me to him had started to sizzle again. I couldn't help myself. He made me go weak at the knees without even trying.

'I've missed you,' his voice was soft. But it was more than mere words. I could see it in his sparkling eyes, which seemed to dilate slightly as he gazed at me. He really had missed me.

'What?' Not the coolest response at that juncture, I agree, but it was the best I could manage. 'I missed you, too,' I tacked one. Although my voice and tone weren't a patch on his, I meant it with all my heart.

Oh, my God, did he just blush? We sipped our wine and just absorbed each other for a while. It was as if the ice had been broken and for the first time, I felt like I didn't have to say or do anything and could just be with him, enjoying the moment. It had turned out to be the perfect Monday evening.

The rest of the week and the weekend passed in a blur of Nicholas. Not that I was complaining, far from it. We hung out together and did stuff that couples did when they dated. Slept, ate, drank, watched movies and danced together and most important of all, talked. It was perfect. I felt sixteen again.

Nicholas had taken me to an art exhibition. The main artist, as it turned out, was the lady Nicholas had recommended to help us with the refurbishment of the Duxton, a Miss Joanne Ong. She was, I guessed, in her early thirties, round faced with a very short, squarish hair style. Her clothes looked like a dog from every village. Meaning her bright yellow blouse, lime green skirt and gold wedge shoes, seemed at odds with each other. But she was the designer, so I guess she had a flair for the unusual.

Now, if I were to be completely honest, which, of course, I always am, within thirty seconds of seeing her work, I could only say that it was a little out there. It was almost as if she had taken a mouthful of paint and then clapped her hands on her cheeks, spewing paint every which way. This description of what I assumed was her technique would come close to what her artworks looked like to me. But what would I know, right?

As it turned out, what I thought of her art was irrelevant, because I liked her personality, it was infectious and warm, and so agreed to hire her. Something I hoped I wouldn't regret.

The next morning, I woke up early, my mind abuzz with thoughts and ideas when the phone rang.

'What are you doing right now?' asked Nicholas's mellifluous voice.

Supine, I stared up at the ceiling. I had been thinking about how we could re-define and enhance the hotel's new brand and image. I felt we were missing something crucial—the need to capture the history of the hotel without making it boring or irrelevant. An elusive thought hovered at the periphery of my mind and evaded all attempts to seize it. The harder I tried, the further it slipped away.

'Nothing,' I said, reluctant to trigger a work-related conversation.

'Well, a friend has invited us over for brunch. Can you come?'

'At what time?' I glanced over at the clock and noted that it was already 9.30 a.m.

'Twelvish?' and quickly added, 'unless you have something else going on today.'

'No, no, I'm free,' I sat up.

'Great.'

No sooner had the word passed his lips than I felt giddy and lightheaded. It was as if I had drunk far too much champagne and the bubbles had gone straight to my heart. I felt dizzy and wonderful. If this was what dating felt like, I loved it. My face almost ached with the wideness of my smile. I hung up the phone in a daze, wondering whether this was all an amazing dream. I repeated to myself, *I'm dating and it's cool.*

A few hours later, Nicholas called to let me know he was in a taxi, outside my Housing Development Board (HDB) apartment block. I ran down to meet him. My powers of observation working on hyperdrive, I noticed he was in a white, linen shirt and, instead of the jeans he usually wore, he was wearing cream-coloured linen trousers with a pair of soft, brown, suede loafers. I couldn't help but break into what I could only imagine was a goofy smile, thinking how lucky I was as I kissed him.

I glanced at my reflection in the taxi's window. I was in a simple silk, oriental, floral-patterned halter-necked top with skinny jeans and black heels. 'Underdressed' was the word I would use.

'Should I change?' I asked.

'Not at all,' he smiled. 'You look perfect.'

That was when I realized that we were officially beginning to feel like a couple who were into each other.

Chapter 14

Nicholas and I had been seeing each other for precisely three weeks. It was still exciting to see him.

We were both sitting in the rear of a taxi, heading home after a nice dinner, and one could say this was a good time to pose a sensitive question, although others may have deemed it better to have have been asked over dinner, where the ambience was romantic and relaxed, and the mood lubricated by several glasses of wine.

My face felt flushed and as red as a tomato. Nicholas was eyeing me anxiously like he was working up the courage to tell me something he thought I may not like to hear.

'I've been thinking,' he started.

'Really? About what?'

Nicholas drew a deep breath and took my hand gently in his. At this point, my innate paranoia tensed with worry. My heart began to race. Was he going to end it? or ask for some time apart? or, perhaps he was bored with me, and expected more? My fingers began to twitch and I groped around my wrist seeking my rubber band. Oh, wait! Perhaps a marriage proposal was in the offing.

'I've been thinking of taking a trip home. To England,' he announced matter-of-factly.

'Oh.' I certainly wasn't expecting that.

'I plan to leave tomorrow night actually.' He sounded normal, just as he should, I guess, although a selfish part of me was hoping to hear a smidgeon of guilt in his voice or see a twinge of remorse in his expression.

'What!?' I squeaked. 'For how long?'

'Just a week; to see the family.' Our eyes locked trying to read each other's reaction. His pupils were not dilated as far as I could tell.

But hang on, the rational side of my brain butted in, *why should I mind? He was a free agent; free to do whatever he wanted.*

'That's nice,' I said, calmly, and smiled.

'Well, I wondered if you would like to come with me actually?' he squeezed my hand gently.

'Me? What?' I think I almost hit the roof of the taxi as I leaped in my seat.

'Yes. So, will you come?'

I let go of his hand and interlaced my fingers worriedly, a sure sign that my anxiety levels were spiralling, although I wasn't sure why because his request clearly indicated his commitment to our relationship and that was simultaneously exciting and scary.

Scientific evidence supports the interconnection between fear of losing control and behaviours that are often characteristic of an obsessive, compulsive disorder. Part of my condition meant that I did, at times, fear losing control and as such I would exhibit checking behaviours. This meant:

(a) I was worried that I would hurt his feelings if I refused and (b) didn't know if I would or could handle it if I agreed.

As if sensing my inner turmoil, he said, 'Relax. It's just a short trip home, and I thought perhaps it would be nice if you came with me and met my family?'

My brain started to process what he had said. Logic told me to mull it over, but I was Clara Tan and most of the time, logic evaded me and my mouth overran my brain.

'I would have to get time off work. It's very short notice, Nicholas.' Great! I had come up with the worst possible reason; one that sounded utterly lame. Even I was kicking myself.

'I'm sure they can spare you for a few days, Clara. Tell Mr Chan you will do some research while in London. I can take you to see a few of the hotels I did the branding for,' which, all things considered, was actually a very good idea. Time to recover a little from my lame attempt to not go.

'So, tell me all about your family,' I said, a hint of excitement in my voice. The night was young, and I was kind of interested to hear all about them.

Chapter 15

My shower routine was wonderful and felt endless. First, I turned on the cold faucet to shock myself awake; then, I gradually increased the temperature and felt the warmth of the water soothe my body. I danced under the fine spray. I plopped a handful of apple-scented shampoo on my crown and worked it into a thick lather, before rinsing it away. I repeated this once more before doing the same with a handful of conditioner. I would have to be at death's door or marooned on a desert island to not wash my hair every day.

My head spun with nonsensical images and I leaned against the tiles, remembering what it was like to lean against Nicholas in the same shower just a few hours ago.

He was making coffee when I entered the kitchen this morning. I was wearing one of his t-shirts as a knee-length dress. I liked that it smelled of him.

He greeted me with a simple, 'Good morning, beautiful,' and beamed that boyish smile. It triggered an immediate flashback and my skin instantly prickled. We were pressed together and when I had glanced sideways, in my peripheral vision I glimpsed his body in the bedside mirror. My heart stuttered when I remembered how it had felt to have his hand cradling my jaw, tilting my chin to meet his mouth. Tasting me like I was something sweet and delicious.

I looked at him as I entered the kitchen. He was looking at my mouth and I knew he was remembering the exact same thing.

'Morning,' I said and sat down on a stool at the breakfast counter. 'So, what's the protocol when we stay with your parents?' I asked without preamble. Memories of last night still danced around in my head.

'Protocol?'

'Yes. Will we sleep in the same room?'

Nicholas cocked his head. 'We'll be in one of the guest rooms. Why?' He passed me a cup of espresso.

'I was just wondering if your parents are conservative about such things. My mother would be.' I took a sip of the coffee and the nutty, almost chocolate, flavours exploded in my palate, 'Mmmm, that's good.'

'Don't worry. Let's just say that they are very down-to-earth folk,' he assured me and turned away. I could see him smiling to himself in his reflection on the kettle. I wondered what being 'down-to-earth' meant. It wasn't a phrase I was familiar with. Nicholas had turned around and was looking back at me, probably wondering what I would make of his parents. My hope was that, if he adored me, they would too.

'You look thoughtful,' I remarked.

'I like the uncomplicated beauty that I can see in your eyes. Does that answer your question?' he replied after a moment.

'Oh wow!' was all I could say. I was brought back to earth when he asked if I had packed.

Of course, I had. But a heavy cloud still hung over me despite the excitement of the trip. What would his parents think of me? Would I be the princess they had hoped their son would meet, or would I be that strange Asian girl they had prayed he would not. My own mother, too, had her own ideations of her ideal son-in-law, and Nicholas certainly didn't fit that bill. So, it would only be fair for me to also disappoint. But too late for that now. In a few short hours we would be at the airport, ready for take-off.

I have never, in all of my twenty-nine-years on this earth, left the safe and protected shores of Singapore, unless you counted a forty-minute ferry ride to the tiny Indonesian island of Batam. Nobody really goes to Batam unless you were a golfer looking for a massage. Which I wasn't. It was a three-day training course in hospitality for me.

My point being: it hardly qualified as an international-travel experience. So, finding myself at Changi Airport about to board a huge aeroplane bound for London, was daunting to say the least. My anxiety levels were in hyperdrive. Imagine trying to pass through immigration, making sure to the millimetre that my passport was aligned squarely in the scanner—much to the sighs and moans of those behind me. Even selecting which sweets to take on board, to enjoy while watching a movie, took me almost twenty minutes. The very concept of watching a movie at 35,000 feet excited me. Not to mention choosing my on-board reading material from the bookstore, which I could only do after I had aligned every book on the shelf perfectly. I was a nightmare, and I had half expected Nicholas to leave me behind. But he had stood by valiantly, watching and smiling. There was only one solution, excessive retail therapy. It would distract me from the nail-biting experience of being locked into a flying bus for almost twelve hours straight, along with over 300 other people, all breathing the same air and expelling the same germs.

I agreed to meet Nicholas at the gate in forty minutes. I couldn't help but see the relief light up his eyes, especially because he had just walked past a bar with the allure of a cold beer. Not to mention he wanted to look for a gift for his parents. We parted and set off on our respective missions.

I caught a reflection of myself in the window of Burberry. I didn't look half bad, but I was going to meet Nicholas's family and would probably not have time to change, should we land safely and live to tell the tale. I was in jeans and a plain white t-shirt from Cotton On, coupled with a little angora cardigan from Marks and Spencer to keep me warm. Drab, yet practical. Perhaps a black, pencil skirt from French Connection teamed with a white blouse would be more classic, but hardly conducive to flying long-haul. Was I going to panic about this as well? No.

At least underneath I had on a new, matching set of bra and panties, embroidered with tiny, pink rosebuds. So, anyway there I was, staring at my reflection and I noticed a red-and-white sign that instantly drew my attention. SALE. My skin prickled with excitement and I could see myself in the raincoat that was so traditionally Burberry. The next thing I knew, I was inside the shop, facing down the assistant who looked at me like I was in the wrong store. Perhaps I didn't look like the typical Tai-Tai shopper with too much Botox and way too much make-up or a Chinese tourist dripping with money. Much to her surprise, having tried on the garment and twirling a couple of times in front of the mirror, my credit card beeped and I was the proud, new owner of a raincoat and scarf. England is cold and wet after all.

'Hi, look I bought some clothes,' I announced far too loudly as I met up with Nicholas at the gate. It was obvious to everyone around us that I was a travel novice and airports were a new experience to me. As always the gentleman, Nicholas smiled and handed me my ticket. To be fair, this was all new and so delightful. It was like several Christmases and birthdays rolled into one. I was over the moon like an excited little girl who had just been given a new doll. Everything was a novelty to me, and I was enjoying myself thoroughly, *and why the hell not?*

As we boarded the plane, Nicholas guided me deftly. I was overwhelmed and rather taken aback by the effusive smiles, charm and friendliness of the cabin crew. As we took our seats in first class, I felt as if I had fallen into some dreamlike fugue. My heart was racing, but this time with excitement, not anxiety. I felt like royalty and had that amazing feeling one had when one sat in a brand-new car and the smell of leather filled one's nostrils. The seats alone were worthy of a moment for pause. They looked like they were straight out of a sci-fi movie. All I could recall of that moment was Nicholas smiling at me and saying, 'Right, let's get you settled in then.' As if it were the most natural thing in the world.

'Is everything okay?' a member of the cabin crew asked.

'It's perfect! Thank you very much.' I mean, what else could I say.

'Great,' she smiled somewhat mechanically and walked away. I suddenly respected the countless times she must give this standard response. Poor woman; but, I guess, that was her job. Being in hospitality myself, I could relate. I pushed my handbag under the seat in front of me and settled back.

Wow. This really was lovely. Big, wide seats and footrests, and everything. This was going to be a completely pleasurable experience from start to finish, I told myself firmly. Nicholas had already started to read an auto magazine and looked right at home.

I buckled my seatbelt nonchalantly, trying to ignore the flutters of apprehension in my stomach. I hadn't flown long-haul before. In fact, I hadn't ever flown before.

'Would you like some champagne?' said the warm, friendly voice of the stewardess.

'That would be great,' I replied, equally warmly. I accepted the flute as it was handed to me. 'Thank you!'

She then turned to Nicholas. 'And for you, sir? Some champagne?'

'Thank you,' he replied without even raising his eyes from his magazine.

'Is it interesting?' I asked him.

'Yes. A man is restoring an old Norton motorcycle,' he replied. Not that I had any idea what that meant. I decided to leave him be. Perhaps this flight was a routine thing to him; whereas for me, it was a thrilling new experience.

We were in the middle column of seats. I caught the glance of the man in the adjacent row; he was in jeans and an old t-shirt emblazoned with some rude word symbolizing his assumption that he had freedom of speech. His eyes were dark, he had a stubble and a deep frown furrowed his brow.

The air hostess asked him if he wanted champagne.

'No thanks. Just a beer,' he replied gruffly. He had a British accent. Realizing that I was looking at him, he turned away and stared out the window.

I returned to my own thoughts. The truth was, I didn't really like this. Flying that is. Being locked in for hours with no escape. I knew it was first class and I knew it was high-end luxury, nevertheless my stomach was clenched in a tight knot of fear. I decided not to bother Nicholas and dwelled on happy thoughts instead.

As we took off, I counted very slowly with my eyes closed, and that kind of worked. I gripped Nicholas's hand and squeezed hard. I ran out of steam at about 250, so I sipped champagne and read an article titled, '30 Things to do Before you're 30', in *Cosmo*. I was trying very hard to look like a seasoned passenger, but, oh God, every tiny sound startled me; every judder made me catch my breath.

'Are you okay?' Nicholas looked up from his reading material, obviously having noticed my incessant twitching.

'Not really. I don't feel good,' I replied. Then with an outward veneer of calm I reached for the laminated safety instructions and pored over them paying close attention to the safety exits, the brace position and the life jackets. It clearly said please assist the elderly and children first. Oh God—if I were going to seek out a small child to help as the plane plummeted down and simultaneously worry about tying the perfect bow on my lifejacket string, it would be catastrophic. And why did the woman in the picture look so happy to be blowing a whistle in a life raft. Wouldn't she be frozen in fear?

'Hey, take it easy. It's fine,' Nicholas reached over and patted my hand.

'I'm trying,' I said dryly.

Why was I even *looking* at this? How would it help to see pictures of little stick people jumping into the ocean while their plane exploded behind them? I quickly stuffed the safety instructions leaflet back into the seat pocket in front of me and took a gulp of champagne.

'Better?'

'Yes. Much.' I was lying of course. Just then, a loud whirring sound rose through the floor and I jumped in my seat.

'What was that?' I asked.

'What?' Nicholas cocked his head, trying to listen for whatever it was that had made me jump.

'That sound. That kind of whining . . . it seems to be coming from the wing.'

'I can't hear anything,' he looked at me sympathetically. 'Don't be nervous. I'm right here with you.'

'No!' I tittered. 'No, I'm not *nervous*! I was just . . . wondering. Just out of interest.'

One of the air hostesses moved past us carrying a tray of drinks, staggering a little as the plane gave a bump. Nicholas got up, gave me a reassuring nod and headed to the washroom.

'Why is the plane bumping?' I asked the stewardess.

Oh God. An unnamed dread seized me. This was sheer madness. Madness! Sitting in this metal tube, with no way of escape, thousands and thousands of feet above the ground . . .

I couldn't do this. Not on my own. An overpowering urge to talk to Nicholas flooded through me. About anything, anything at all. I needed to feel safe and take my mind off it. I snapped my millionth rubber band.

Instinctively, I reached for my mobile phone. The air hostess swooped down on me. 'I'm afraid you can't use that on board the plane,' she said apologetically with her bright fixed smile. 'Please make sure it's switched off.'

'Oh. Sorry,' I apologized, feeling a bit stupid. Of course, I couldn't use my mobile. They had only said it about fifty-five zillion times. I was such a duh. Anyway, never mind. It didn't really matter. I was fine. I put the phone away in my bag and tried to concentrate on the film that was playing on the in-flight entertainment system—a Jennifer Aniston starrer that I had wanted to watch for ages.

Perhaps I should start counting again, I mused. At least until Nicholas came back. *349, 350, 3*— My head jerked up. Was that a thump? Did we just get *hit*? Okay, don't panic, I told myself.

It was just a jar. I assured myself that everything was just fine. We had probably flown into a pigeon or something. Now where was I?

351, 352, 35—And that was it. That was the moment that everything seemed to fragment and my mind started to hallucinate, imagining all the worst-case scenarios I could think of. I heard the screaming break out like a tidal wave over my head almost before I realized what was happening.

Oh God. Oh God, oh God, oh God, oh . . . OH . . . NO. NO. NO. We were falling. Oh God, we were falling. We were plummeting in a tail spin. The plane was dropping like a stone through the air. A man over there shot into the air and banged his head on the ceiling. He was bleeding. I was gasping, clutching my seat, trying not to do the same thing, but I could feel myself being wrenched upwards, like someone was physically tugging at me, like a switch had been thrown and gravity had suddenly been reversed. There was no time to think.

My mind couldn't . . . cabin baggage whirled around us, drinks were spilled, one of the cabin crew had fallen over and she clutched at a seat to stay anchored . . . *Oh God. Oh God.*

Okay, it was slowing down now and righting itself. It was . . . it was better. Okay. It was . . . it was kind of . . . back to normal now.

'Ladies and gentlemen,' a voice crackled over the intercom. 'This is your captain speaking.'

My heart started to judder in my chest. I couldn't bear to listen. I couldn't think.

'We have hit some clear-air turbulence and things may be unsteady for a while. I have switched on the fasten-seatbelt signs and would ask that you all return to your seats as quickly as you can.'

'Hi! You okay?' asked Nicholas, sliding into his seat as calm as you like. 'It's just a little turbulence. Keep calm; it will soon pass.'

Keep calm? I couldn't breathe, forget '*keep calm*'. What were we going to do? Were we all supposed to just *sit* here while the plane bucked like an out-of-control bronco?

I could hear someone behind me reciting, 'Hail Mary, full of grace . . .' and a fresh surge of choking panic swept through me. People were praying. This was real. We were going to die. We were going to die. *Did I just say that out loud?*

'We are going to die.' I stared into Nicholas's face. This could be the last person I ever saw alive. I drank in his eyes and his strong jaw, shaded with stubble.

'No. Clara, I don't think we're going to die,' he sounded unbelievably confident. Then everything stopped and we were back to normal. 'See? I told you,' he patted me again.

'I need some sleep. This has all been a bit much.'

Chapter 16

I squinted as the sunlight shone in my face through the aircraft's oval window. We had moved to two vacant seats across the aisle and I had the window seat. Now, I could see that beyond the thin, protective plastic was a landscape of fluffy, white clouds and clear, blue skies. Below, between the breaks in the carpet of clouds, our landfall could be seen, but it was impossible to tell where we were because, at this distance, everything seemed so minuscule. To me it was an amazing sight and worthy of the effort I had expended to force my eyes open.

'Hi,' I felt Nicholas gently tug at my hand.

'Hi, handsome,' I replied and then stretched and sat up a little.

'Champagne?' Nick offered me a flute. It was chilled to the touch and the tiny bubbles inside were almost mesmerizing.

'Thanks. I could get used to this.' I already had, in truth, but I wasn't about to tell him.

'So, are you looking forward to meeting my crazy family?' he asked.

'Yes, of course,' I replied. 'Tell me about them again; it was nice to hear.'

'Sure.' I sipped my champagne and settled back. 'Well, you may remember that Sally, my sister, has a great sense of humour.'

'Yes.' I said.

'Well, she uses it to help cope with her OCD. She acknowledges her obvious compulsions, like tapping and touching. She pokes fun at herself most of the time which makes everyone around her feel more comfortable, I guess. That bit I didn't tell you last time.'

'No, you didn't. Why not?'

'Personal I guess.'

'When did you first know she had the condition?' I asked.

'She was in her early teens when we first noticed her obsessive thoughts. She couldn't figure out why they were happening or what was going on. She had a couple of different ones that rotated. One was that she was going to fall asleep while eating her dinner. Another was that she was going to drop her house keys in a drain. Another was that she was going to trip over her shoe laces while walking.'

'Oh, goodness,' I muttered. Not because I was shocked, but I was starting to really relate to Sally.

'Poor thing, She started to fear the thoughts so much that she would avoid doing things that we all normally did. She would avoid manholes and bend down every few yards to make sure her shoe laces were tied. I lost count of how many times she used to do that on a simple walk to the shops.'

I almost said OMG out loud. Now it all made sense. That was why he empathized with me. His own sister was just like me and I hadn't known this. Why hadn't he told me that before? I answered myself: *why should he?* And he had just told me it was too personal.

'I see. Good for her,' a lame response considering my actual surprise.

'Yeah. She can be a little nuts. Like, she has to brush her teeth five times a day,' he laughed.

'Well, you know I can relate to it, so thank you for sharing.'

'Yes, I thought you would.'

'And your brothers, John and Mike? I remember you telling me about them,' I prompted him.

'Yes, John and Mike. A pair of characters. They are both clones of my father. Strong-minded, stubborn and a bit crude. So, be warned. I take after Mum thankfully.'

'Crude? You didn't tell me that,' I wanted to know more.

'Bad language, dirty jokes, that kind of thing,' Nicholas almost blushed with embarrassment. 'Second thoughts . . . I think we should ask the captain to turn back. You . . . meeting my family . . . not a good idea,' he chuckled weakly.

'Hey. It's okay. They can be themselves,' I really didn't mind. Being the only child in a single-parent household, to me, having any kind of a large family, would be better than not. Besides, they sounded fun.

'And your mother? What's she like again?' I reached over and took his hand.

'Mum is a whirlwind of energy. In your face all the time, so be prepared. Like I said, she runs the family, make no mistake,' he was serious, I could tell.

'Dad, as I said, is smart, street-wise, successful, but raw. But my mother is on a whole other level. She can read people like a book.'

A thrum of anxiety coursed through me as I recalled my illogical fear of his mother summarily rejecting my suit. Another swig of champagne was needed. Which was well timed because the overly, made-up air hostess just happened by with a super-chilled bottle. I refilled my glass and settled back in my seat. What I needed now was a movie, something to take my mind off the impending meeting with his family. Something like *Meet the Fockers*. Just perfect, I thought.

Chapter 17

We arrived at Heathrow at seven the next morning. As I peered out of the airplane's window, I immediately knew that we were in the UK. How? It was a gloomy morning—either that or the sun was clearly still asleep. As we ambled towards immigration, Nicholas made the effort to point out the things of difference. I learnt that Heathrow was not Changi because there wasn't a single tropical plant in sight or a fish pond bursting with koi. Everything looked tired and old. It was a far cry from the sterile, ultra-modern terminal we had departed from.

Having collected our luggage, which took an eternity, and exited through customs, little could have prepared me for what was to come.

No sooner than we emerged through the automatic doors, I heard a loud, strident voice almost screaming, shortly followed by Nicholas being swept off his feet by a woman I could only hope was his mother. Which fortunately, I found out later, it was. He looked fragile in his mother's arms as she spun him around. Without being rude, she was a large and powerful woman, almost along the lines of a grizzly bear, and I freely admit I froze in my tracks.

'You must be Clara?' came a voice from behind me. I turned around to see a man standing there, smiling. 'Don't mind her, love, she misses her boy,' he said and held out his arms as if offering a hug. At that point, I made another assumption that the man, now wanting to embrace me, was Jack, Nicholas's father. What the hell, I thought, and sank into the embrace.

'I'm Clara,' I announced, which was silly because he already knew that. He hugged me affectionately as if I were his own daughter, which, I thought, was kind of nice and a good start to the trip.

'I'll get your bags,' he said.

It was then my turn to be flung around like a ragdoll, as I felt a pair of powerful arms wrap around me and lift me effortlessly skyward.

'Here, let me have a look at you. Let's see what my boy has brought me,' said Maureen as if I were a box of chocolates and brought as a gift.

'Careful, Mum. Clara's delicate,' said Nicholas.

'Oh, don't be silly, dear, I'll be gentle.'

Little did she realize I was struggling to breathe, but I managed to splutter out a 'Hi, Maureen,' before being set back on terra firma.

'You're nervous, dear, no need. I'll take care of you.' It was true it seemed. She could read people like books. I was indeed nervous.

I took them both in for a moment as they returned to fussing over Nicholas and suddenly understood why he had missed them so much. They seemed so warm and genuine, which made me relax. I had been dreading their not making me feel welcome, but I had no need to worry—I felt very welcome.

'Now, let's get you both home for a nice cup of tea. You bring the bags Jack,' Maureen commanded, before we were all herded towards the main entrance, like lost lambs.

As we reached the car park and Jack retrieved his car keys from his coat pocket, I was in for another shock. I was expecting a BMW or even a simple Toyota, certainly not a Rolls Royce. I think the fact that my mouth was gaping wide gave my level of surprise away.

'You didn't tell me you were rich,' I tugged at Nicholas and whispered into his ear.

'I guess we're comfortable as a family, yes, but it's not my money.' He appeared to take it all in his stride.

Jack, who seemed to have heard me, merely commented, 'It's just a car, love. Drinks petrol like a camel.'

All the same, it was, in my opinion, more than 'just a car'. At home it would be a couple of HDB apartments at least.

As we made our way to their home which, I was told, was in a place called Bromley, in the county of Kent, I gazed out of the window and took in the countryside, the hedgerows, fields and little villages, like I had never seen anything like them before. Which, in fact, I hadn't. It was a far cry from the HDB blocks of Singapore. Everything looked so tiny and pretty. For the first time I realized why people called everything in England 'quaint'.

'Not far now,' said Nicholas, as we arrived at yet another junction of crossroads. 'We make a right down here, then a left and then straight on for another mile although it feels like we've been driving forever.'

'Oh, this arrived for you this morning, boy,' Jack handed an envelope over his shoulder, skilfully continuing to navigate the Rolls along the now very narrow roads.

Nicholas opened the envelope to reveal a wedding invitation. He held it so that I could read it too.

'Gilbert James and Jenny Stuart request the pleasure of your company . . .'

I read over his shoulder, fascinated by the exquisite calligraphy. 'Good friends of yours?' I asked.

'More like family, really. Gilbert is my cousin. They've been going out for well over a year now. Gilbert basically moved into the flat I used to share with him before I left for Singapore—although they seem to be spending more and more time in Scotland these days. That's where Jenny is from. They're both very sweet and laid back, and everyone has agreed that they make a brilliant couple,' he said to give me a quick synopsis of their background, which I thought was nice.

'They sound great,' I said and then fell silent. My eyeballs had just popped out on stalks. The monumental home of the Tate family came into view as we turned into what some would call a road but was, in fact, the driveway to their home. Even some of Singapore's elite would do a double take at this mansion. 'Oh, my God. Is that—'

'It's our little palace, dear,' said Maureen. We continued down the long and wide sweep of driveway lined with giant oak trees that culminated in a circular gravel portico. The house was large, grey and ancient-looking, with creeper-covered pillars at the front.

'Little? It looks like Buckingham Palace,' I had to say it and I probably sounded like a yokel.

'No, dear. It's Downe Hall, certainly not Buckingham Palace,' I think Maureen thought I was being serious. 'We snatched it off some toffee-nosed lord about ten years ago for a song. Isn't that right, Jack?'

Jack nodded as he pulled up at the front door.

'I'm glad you like it,' said Nicholas.

'It's bigger than the Duxton.' I felt like a fish out of water, although that didn't deter me from immediately Instagramming pictures to both Loretta and Ken. 'How old is it?' I asked.

'Dunno,' said Nicholas vaguely. 'All I know is that it was in the previous owner's family for years. He had to sell it when the stock market crashed in 2008.'

'Yeah, Stupid prick. His loss, our gain,' said Jack caustically.

I froze as I felt a wave of anxiety engulf me. I had completely forgotten that Nicholas had brothers and a sister, and there they were, waiting for us, all lined up outside the house, like a scene from *Downton Abbey*. My heartrate speeded up as I climbed out of the car and approached them, somewhat timidly. It could go one of two ways, I thought, either I froze and looked like a complete imbecile, or their faces would reveal the fact that they didn't like me . . . I breathed slowly to calm myself and prevent any further negative thoughts. Nicholas brushed past me to embrace his siblings. I could see immediately that they adored him. Then, it was my turn. I eased forward.

'Hi, I'm Clara,' I said, with as much confidence as I could muster.

As it turned out, Sally, was delightful and greeted me European style with a kiss on each cheek. As if following her example, both

John and Mike showered me with hugs and kisses, too. I lost count of how many.

I said, 'Thank you of course.'

'So, Clara, I take it my brother is keeping you happy in the love department?' Mike said with a wink.

'Mike, please.' Nicholas blushed immediately.

'Well, he is hung like a donkey,' John joined in.

'Ignore them, Clara. Boys!' Sally said.

'You're as crude as your father,' Maureen interjected.

'Yup, chips off the old block,' Jack guffawed.

For the next hour, I was shown around Downe Hall by Maureen and Sally. I lost count of how many bedrooms, bathrooms, study areas and various other rooms it had. But the west wing, which sounded grand enough on its own, was where we were to stay.

Maureen, with the aid of a lady who I assumed was her housekeeper, had disappeared into the kitchen to fix high tea and I took the time to get to know Sally. We exchanged countless stories and made an immediate connection. She thought it hilarious that I was wondering where all the household servants were. Sally was very sweet, in that she politely explained to me that only the queen had such staff these days, and they made do with an elderly lady from the village who helped Maureen run the house. But, I did learn that they had a gardener too. I also got to observe how alike Sally and I actually were, when she arranged the spoons in the cutlery drawer in the kitchen and washed her hands every thirty minutes or so. I would have done exactly the same.

'So how is it for you?' she asked. 'The OCD.'

'I cope,' I replied.

'Yes. I know what you mean. At the age of twelve, I remember almost being in tears as I wrote, erased and rewrote my name countless times at the top of my homework, aiming for a perfection that my brain only allowed out of sheer exhaustion. And, being raised Catholic, I used to repeat rosary after rosary and prayer after prayer out of fear I hadn't prayed enough,' she laughed.

'Oh, my God, I used to do the same thing. The name-writing thing,' I said. We hugged each other. It was so good to talk to someone who could understand me at long last.

'Yes. When I feel a bit out of control, that OCD side of my brain thinks it can settle things down and control things by fussing about with writing everything perfectly and neatly or making sure I hang my shirt a certain way. OCD is such an odd loop to unwind from, don't you think?' I could certainly identify with her and we talked for hours. Which was fortunate as Nicholas had retired with his father and brothers to the billiard room and was happily catching up. It was great to see him with his family whom he had clearly missed.

After the grand tour of the home, I was impressed by the array of family photographs, some of which showed Nicholas looking slightly awkward in woollen jumpers knitted by, I suspect, his grandmother.

Sally led the way as we entered a huge, flagstone-floored hall, where a Labrador lay fast asleep by a crackling fire. It was so picturesque, and I felt like I was in some British sitcom. The room was comfortably furnished with sofas and armchairs, with soft rugs scattered on the floor.

Having had high tea and listened to the endless stories about Nicholas when he was little, I hit the wall as jet lag came calling. My eyes refused to stay open even a second longer.

Nicholas carried me to bed and we collapsed together on a king-size bed in the west wing.

Tomorrow would be the start of a whole new adventure in the world of the Tates. But I felt so welcome and accepted. They hadn't made me feel like an intrusive interloper. This was just perfect.

Chapter 18

The morning started with a huge breakfast: eggs, bacon, sausages, baked beans and mushrooms. Maureen told me that this was what was known as a 'full English breakfast'.

'So, what are your plans today?' Maureen asked as she delivered a refilled pot of tea to the table.

'I thought a day out in the city would be good,' said Nicholas, 'show Clara the sights.'

'Buckingham Palace,' I piped up. I had seen innumerable post cards and TV shows about the palace where the queen lived. How cool was that? It seemed so grand that I wanted to see it for myself. It was so thoroughly 'English' in my view. It was the first thing that most tourists thought of.

'Sure, why not?' Nicholas laughed.

'Well, enjoy yourselves. Just let me know if you need dinner,' said Maureen. 'If not, I'll take your father down to the pub for fish and chips.'

'Thanks. I think we'll eat in town, so you go ahead.' He kissed her on the cheek and then turned to me. 'Come on, let's get ready and we can get going.'

I finished my mouthful of sausage. 'Sure.'

Now that our plan for the day was set, I finished my tea and tagged along behind Nicholas like an obedient puppy. I felt rather stuffed after the enormous breakfast and couldn't help wondering whether I would continue to eat like this all week.

As we neared London an hour or so later, my mind started to anticipate the experience ahead.

Fog. London always seemed to be shrouded in fog, at least in all the movies and storybooks and sitcoms; and there were red buses everywhere and taxis that looked like lines of black ants as they swarmed through the traffic. Fried food and smelly sewers.

Now, stop Clara. It will be more like rose gardens and green parks with lakes filled with ducks.

In actual fact, I had no idea what to expect and my imagination ran riot. I would just have to wait and see it all for myself. In any case, I was with Nicholas, on cloud nine, and that was all that mattered. What we did or what I thought of London was inconsequential.

It was not long before we were riding a black cab that was threading its way through the narrow streets. The city seemed to wrap itself around me like a concrete blanket. The buildings looked old and grey, not at all like the architectural newness of Singapore's central business district. Yet, sprinkled among the old buildings, I could see modern edifices of blue, smoked glass and steel and even skyscrapers that reached for the sky. Old-meets-new formed this new environment that unfolded before my astonished eyes.

I observed the people, who seem to be walking at a fast pace, unlike the lethargic and relaxed gait of the people back home. This was probably because of the heat and humidity in Singapore. It was all so very different here. It felt for a moment that I was in a parallel universe with everything just a tad more vivid.

Although Nicholas hadn't exactly told me where we were going and what we would see, other than Buckingham Palace, I felt calm. No knots in the stomach or desire to twang my rubber band.

Perhaps he would take me to a museum or an art gallery. I mean, I liked art, but my attention span lasted about five minutes at the most in front of a picture. As for a museum, God, I hoped not!

I would rather stick cocktail sticks in my eyeballs. Not my cup of tea at all. I rather think I owed this aversion to my mother's having dragged me, willy-nilly, every Sunday, to the Singapore history museum on Sentosa Island. It had dusty old mannequins in Peranakan outfits, frozen in a tableau as they pushed carts loaded with spices, depicting a scene from back in the day when Boat Quay was the hub of Singapore's trading. I mean, it was important and all that, but the times had moved on.

Perhaps Nicholas would take me for lunch at one of those la-di-dah high-falutin places where one's meal, when served, was concealed beneath a silver cloche, and there were a million knives and forks to use and snooty waiters looked superciliously down their noses at you, just waiting to catch you out doing something utterly countrified. *Pretty Woman*, the scene where Julia Roberts shoots a snail across the restaurant sprang to mind.

'I thought we would just have a nice, simple lunch later,' said Nicholas, looking over at me. It was as if he could read my mind.

'Lovely,' I breathed, 'sounds just perfect.' Thank goodness. That probably meant we were not going anywhere stuffy. No, we were going to some tiny, tucked-away place that hardly anyone knew about. Some little Italian restaurant for pizza or pasta. The kind of place where one knocked on an anonymous-looking door in a back alley and when one got inside, it would be bursting at the seams with celebrities behaving like normal people. Yes! And perhaps Nicholas knew them all!

But of course, he knew them all. He was in marketing.

'Hyde Park. We are here,' Nicholas announced. 'You can drop us off here, mate,' he said to the taxi driver and then grinned at me.

'Great,' I said and reached for the door. It wasn't like I had a clue about where we were. As I alighted, I looked around, wondering where on earth we were going.

'We're at Hyde Park Corner,' said Nicholas again.

'What's at Hyde Park Corner?' I turned around slowly to look at the surroundings.

'I thought,' said Nicholas, at my side, 'we could get a bite to eat first, build up some energy and then explore until we drop after.'

'Sounds good.'

After a few minutes of walking, we ducked into a cul-de-sac and slipped in through the backdoor of a building and walked through kitchens, while busy chefs pretended we were invisible, and then we emerged into the foyer of somewhere dark. It looked a lot like a Mafia scene in a film. It just needed someone screaming blue murder in the kitchen as they had the life beaten out of them.

But this was so cool, I thought. We were in an Italian restaurant. I could smell mouth-watering aromas everywhere and it made me ravenous.

'Welcome Mr Nick. Nice to see you again.' The voice that came from behind us had a distinct Italian accent. A tall man, who looked quintessentially Italian, stood with his hands clasped together.

'Salvatore, my old friend,' Nicholas proceeded to kiss him on the cheek. Which seemed odd, but perhaps that was what you did in London. I was then kissed on both cheeks by this handsome stranger.

'Mr Nick. She is every inch the beauty you described. Welcome, Clara.' As far as I was concerned, he could do no wrong after that.

We were shown to a nice little table by the window by a waiter in a starched, white apron and presented with the menus.

'Drinks?' he asked.

'A gin and tonic, please,' I said jokingly and looked at Nicholas, assuming that he would be shocked. Well, it was only noon.

But he grinned gamely and said, 'Unless you want champagne?'

'Oh,' I said, completely thrown.

'I always think champagne and pizza is an excellent combination,' he looked at the waiter. 'A bottle of Dom Pérignon, please.'

Well, this was more like it. This was certainly a lot more like it. Champagne and pizza.

Despite the champagne, which was nice, just being with Nicholas was all that mattered, and we could have been drinking tap water for all I cared. I began to allow in a few thoughts of our future, or what

I hoped would be our future. A happy vision of our wedding day. Me in some wonderful dress; didn't have to be designer, just a simple dress would do. My mum looking on proudly. Just by imagining such a future, I almost felt faint with longing.

The next few hours passed in a flash. Multiple dishes of pasta, fish and meats arrived. The champagne flowed a little too freely, and I began to feel a little tipsy. Nicholas explained to me over lunch that he had done some work for the restaurant a few years ago, which boosted its reputation and ever since, he got to eat here for free.

'I wanted to say—' I started.

'Do you—' he began.

We had both spoken simultaneously.

'Sorry,' I said. 'You go on.'

'No, *you* go on,' said Nicholas.

'Oh . . . I was just going to say thank you for bringing me here and allowing me to stay with your family. I am absolutely loving it.'

'It's my pleasure and Mum and Dad like you,' he smiled.

'They do?' Knowing that greatly helped forestall any onset of anxiety.

'Yes, they do.'

I felt myself blush, my cheeks grew warm. 'You were going to ask me something?' I prompted.

'Oh. Yes. Do you ever wish you had lived in another country? I mean, you haven't I assume,' he smiled.

'No. Singapore is home. But I would love to travel more in the future,' I replied.

'I will see what I can do then,' he said.

We eventually made it out of the restaurant and embarked on what I could only describe as a roller-coaster ride of all London had to offer. It was a blur of the tower of London, Buckingham Palace, Westminster Abbey, Big Ben, Saint Paul's, Trafalgar Square, the Strand, Leicester Square and Covent Garden. We even managed to pop in and see the Savoy and Mandarin Oriental hotels, where Nicholas provided me with chapter and verse of how he helped brand them. I got to see it all, as it passed before my eyes in a kaleidoscopic blur. Taxis and buses and even a boat on the Thames whirled us around the sights.

It came to an end, late in the afternoon when Jenny and Gilbert were to meet us at Harrods. I must admit I was a little anxious as I greeted them, knowing full well that they were Nicholas's loved ones. But they seemed welcoming enough and we all embraced like long-lost friends. I guessed I had passed muster because I was left alone with Jenny to shop while Nicholas and Gilbert headed off for a shave and a haircut.

After three hours, having overspent on my credit card on presents for Mum, Loretta and Ken, I begged to sit down.

'D'you like horses, Clara?' Jenny asked out of the blue. It felt like being asked by a virtual stranger what I thought about world politics. Nonetheless, I smiled sweetly and essayed a reply.

'Horses? I guess so. I've not really thought about it,' I replied as fully as I felt I could. What I wanted to say was, what kind of a question is that? But I refrained.

'Then we should go riding together when you come up to Scotland for our wedding.' Ah! So, that was the reason she had asked. Perhaps it would have been better to have provided that minor detail, before hitting me with it out the blue.

'What a wonderful idea!' I exclaimed. My tone, I thought, gave me away, so I infused some more enthusiasm with, 'That . . . would be such fun!'

God, shut up, Clara. Dig the hole deeper, why don't you! There was no way anyone was getting me on a horse. Not even in Scotland. But that was okay. I would just go along with the plan for now and then, on the day, say I had twisted my ankle or something.

'Do you like dogs?' Jenny asked next.

'I love dogs,' I replied confidently. Which was sort of true. I wouldn't in truth like to own a dog—too much hard work and hairs everywhere. Not to mention having to pick up their poo. Nonetheless, I liked seeing Labradors loping across the East Coast Park back home and cute little puppies . . . that kind of thing.

We lapsed into a moment of silence and I took a few sips of my coffee.

'Do you like *East Enders*?' Jenny asked.

'I've never watched it, I'm afraid,' I said apologetically. 'I'm sure it's very good.'

'Not really,' she said and we both laughed. Nicholas and Gilbert appeared at that moment looking sharp with their new haircuts and baby-smooth faces.

'Right, who's hungry?' Nicholas asked and received a unanimous yes from all of us. A half hour or so later, seated in one of the many cafés within Harrods, finishing off a delightful bowl of clam chowder, Jenny moved Nicholas aside and slipped into the space beside me. Nicholas excused himself to visit the washroom along with Gilbert.

'Do you have any secrets? You know, things you haven't told anyone,' Jenny whispered.

'Yes. I guess so.'

'You do?' she sounded surprised.

'I do. Everyone has a secret or two, don't they? It's completely normal. I'm sure I don't have any more than anybody else.' Not that I was talking about any earth-shattering secrets like *the president of Singapore must eat vanilla ice cream at midnight or he turns into an alien*-type secrets, just normal ones, everyday little secrets. Like for example:

1. My LV speedy bag is a fake from Chinatown
2. I love vodka and have a bottle hidden underneath my bed, so Mum won't find out
3. I thought the capital of Iceland was Paris when I was eight
4. I lost my virginity to a boy called Luke, while Mum was playing Mahjong in the front room with her friends
5. Sometimes, when I'm right in the middle of passionate sex with Nicholas, I suddenly want to brush his hair
6. Mum's blue dress that she loved so much, went mysteriously missing one day. It had accidentally fallen off the drying pole

when I was retrieving the laundry, fell fourteen floors to the ground and was chewed by a dog

7. Mum thinks I love her Hokkien fried noodles. I don't; they taste like feet

8. When my colleague, Ken, really annoys me, I put salt in his tea (which is pretty much every day)

I stopped and asked Jenny, 'Do you have any?'

The surreptitious glance that she flicked towards Gilbert and Nicholas, to see if they were listening, probably meant that she did. I suddenly felt profoundly uncomfortable about prying and wished I could retract the question. Too late. She moved in, very close, almost climbing into my lap.

'I'm pregnant,' she whispered.

'OH MY GOD!' I am pretty sure that everyone in the café heard me. I was the cynosure of all eyes.

Why on earth would she tell me, a complete stranger at that? My mouth was wide open and catching flies.

'No one knows, Clara,' squeaked Jenny, her voice held a distinct note of hysteria.

Feeling flustered, I pushed the hair off my face and tried to get a grip. Okay, let's think of a way to defuse this now very awkward situation.

I closed my eyes to help channel the cerebral juices. What would Loretta do in this situation? But my mind was still giddy from all the champagne at lunch and my thoughts were fragmented. Secrets . . . people's secrets . . .

Nicholas and Gilbert had joined us. Jesus, they must have heard me shriek. Emily then appeared, scowling at me. No, now is not the time Emily. I wiped her away.

Scotland. Suddenly a coherent thought flashed into my mind. I opened my eyes, feeling a tingle of exhilaration.

'Baby,' I declared. 'My baby loves the outdoors. Don't you Nicholas?'

'Baby? You never call me that,' said Nicholas in patent surprise.

'I just thought it would be cute,' out of the corner of my eye I could see Jenny looking askance at me.

'Okay.' Nicholas shrugged and went back to chatting with Gilbert.

'I'm so sorry, Clara. I didn't mean to put you on the spot. Thank you,' Jenny hugged me. 'You're my new best friend.'

An hour or so later, having said our goodbyes, Nicholas and I strolled back to the train station, arm in arm. Nicholas looked preoccupied.

'Are you worrying about something?' I asked.

'Yes. That baby comment . . . Jenny's pregnant, isn't she?'

I did promise Jenny that I wouldn't tell anyone. But . . . Nicholas . . . he was my boyfriend. Shouldn't he know, too? Gilbert was his cousin after all. But I had promised Jenny that I wouldn't tell. Oh, it wasn't like it would change anything now, would it?

'Yes, she is. She asked me not to say anything. Most awkward.'

'Oh, wow! You covered that up well,' Nicholas said drily.

'Not angry with me?'

'Angry. No, why would I be? It's not your fault that she is pregnant. They should both be happy.'

'Yes. I guess so,' our conversation petered out into a pensive silence.

'So . . . does Gilbert wear a chest wig?' I coughed.

'A chest wig!' Nicholas gave an explosive snort of laughter.

'Or a toupée?' I snickered.

'Of course, he doesn't wear a chest wig. *Or* a toupée,' he retorted.

As we boarded the train back home, I made some firm resolutions for the remainder of my stay in England: I would not let anyone stress me out; or mention the words baby or marriage.

I looked at my watch, wondering how soon I could leave for the airport. Hopefully the next few days would be better.

Chapter 19

It had been two days since arriving in London, two days that I had enjoyed thoroughly. To add to my globe-trotting adventure, we then set off for Scotland which, according to the movie, *Braveheart*, is the land of the free. We were on our way to Jenny and Gilbert's wedding.

As we all stepped out of the plane, I wondered whether everyone would be in kilts? I know that sounds incredibly naive, but it was what we, as tourists, expected. Red-headed men with hairy legs, strong arms and strange accents.

But no. Everyone looked fairly normal, like the people in London. For me, however, it was another round of introductions and desperately hoping that I would feel as welcome as I did down south.

I felt I knew both the bride and groom pretty well by now with the rundown provided by Sally while we were driving to Jenny's home from the airport. I knew all about the flat that Jenny and Gilbert were buying in London and I had seen pictures of the gorgeous hotel in Bora Bora where Jenny and Gilbert were going for their honeymoon. I almost felt like an extended member of the family. Gosh! How nice.

Upon our arrival at what resembled a clone of Buckingham Palace, I stood staring in wide-eyed wonder at the sheer magnificence of the house. Nicholas and I were ushered into a very large room in the top floor of the east wing, overlooking a lake—Nicholas told me that it was a 'loch' and not a lake.

A roaring fire blazed and crackled in the fireplace that made the room toasty and warm. Which was fortunate as the central heating in such a large home had little effect. It was all so incredibly romantic, I thought, and the massive four-poster bed in the middle of the room—the size of my entire apartment in Singapore—only added to the ambience of a Gothic, historical romance. I felt dwarfed by the gargantuan proportions of everything here. Singapore had nothing like this, at least not in my part of the island. Gosh, was my naiveté showing?

As we settled in over the next few hours, I observed the comings and goings. Florists laden with flowers, caterers and relatives arrived almost every minute. Endless pots of tea and mounds of fruit cake were ferried to the drawing room as people reunited, chatted and discussed the next few days.

Dogs, both large and small, feasted on the leftovers of cake and endless stream of sandwiches. Which I knew to be very bad. One little dog, named Sprout, a Jack Russell breed I was told, seemed to fancy people's legs. He constantly attached himself and made out. Nicholas just politely pulled him off which, I must admit, was rather comical to watch, however, Jack gave a sharp whack to the dog's snout, sending the poor little thing off whimpering. I felt like I was looking on from some parallel universe, unobserved by those around me. Nicholas and Jack had gone off to explore the grounds, leaving me to my own devices. Not that I minded. It gave me time to unwind and relax.

The next morning, although both Nicholas and I slept like logs, on account of the highland air, we were startled awake by the sound of voices and banging of suitcases from the hallway. It appeared that more people had arrived. Today was the day of the wedding and as we went downstairs for breakfast, everything looked wonderful. The place was redolent with the fragrance of fresh flowers.

I later discovered that I had been invited to join the bridesmaids for a free makeover by some fantastic make-up artist. Who was I to turn that opportunity down? The only downside was that the photographer took countless pictures of me getting made up, which was rather embarrassing. One of the bridesmaids went so far as to suggest that he should perhaps focus on the bride and leave us alone.

I looked over at Jenny who was debating with her mother about which of the six family tiaras she would wear, while she took big gulps of champagne. I couldn't help but feel annoyed, drinking while pregnant was a big no-no. I felt the need to say something.

'Jenny, perhaps you would prefer some juice or something?' I said, looking meaningfully at her stomach.

'Oh, yes, perhaps you're right.'

'Now, time for your mother to have her hair done,' said the hairdresser to Jenny and moved over to Jenny's mother, Caroline, and started to pull and tug at her hair.

'Does she want a blow-dry?' the hairdresser asked.

'I doubt it,' said Jenny, pulling a surprised face. 'She's not really into that kind of stuff.'

'What's she wearing?' the hairdresser asked.

'I'm right here, you know,' said Caroline plaintively, which was rather hilarious.

'The first thing that comes to hand, probably,' Jenny replied wryly. Jenny met my eye and I pulled a sympathetic face.

The previous night, Caroline had come downstairs for drinks in a pair of thick, green, corduroy trousers and a patterned, woollen jumper, with a large, diamond brooch pinned to the front. Mind you, Gilbert's mother looked even worse.

Jenny looked around and noticed that her mother had vanished. 'Clara, be a darling, would you, and go find my mother. Make sure she doesn't put on some hideous old gardening dress? Or her hunting clothes,' and added, 'she'll listen to you, I know she will.'

'Well . . . okay,' I replied doubtfully, not really understanding why her mother would listen to me. 'I'll try.'

As I let myself out of the room, I saw Nicholas coming down the corridor in his suit, looking very handsome and dashing.

'You look beautiful,' he said with a smile.

'Do I?' I did a little twirl for his benefit. 'It's just a simple dress. I wasn't expecting to attend a grand wedding.'

'I wasn't looking at the dress,' he said. His eyes met mine with a wicked glint and I felt a deep thrill of pleasure. 'Is Jenny decent?' he asked. 'I just wanted to wish her well.'

'Oh, yes,' I said, waving him in. 'Go on in. Hey, Nicholas, you look great, too.' I caught his smile as he entered the room.

I eventually made my way to Jenny's mother's bedroom without getting lost in the maze of hallways and knocked gently at her door.

'Yes, what is it?' thundered a voice from within. The door was flung open by Caroline, her weather-beaten face creasing into a broad smile when she saw me.

'Clara!' she boomed and looked at her watch. 'Not time yet, is it?'

'Not quite! Jenny was wondering where you had gotten to.' I smiled hesitantly and cast my eyes over her outfit which was an old, navy-blue sweatshirt, jodhpurs and riding boots. But she did have an amazing figure for a woman her age. No wonder Jenny was so lissom. I glanced around the room for tell-tale signs of a new dress hanging somewhere or hatboxes. There were none.

'I don't need some hairdresser fumbling around me, so, I left.' She turned away into the room. I stepped in behind her.

'So, um, Caroline . . . I was just wondering what you were planning to wear today. As mother of the bride!'

'Mother of the bride?' she stared in surprise. 'Good God, I suppose I am. Hadn't thought of it like that.'

'Right! So, you . . . haven't got a special outfit ready?'

'Bit early to be dressing up, isn't it?' she said. 'I'll just fling something on before we go.'

'Well, why don't I help you choose?' I said firmly and went to the wardrobe. I threw open the doors, inwardly preparing myself for a shock—and gaped in astonishment. This had got to be the most extraordinary collection of clothes I had ever seen. Riding clothes, ball dresses, hunting camo and two-piece suits jostled for space with Indian saris, Mexican ponchos . . . and an extraordinary array of tribal jewellery. I almost wondered whether I had opened the doors to a fancy-dress outfitter. It triggered the autopilot mode of my OCD and I started to arrange things in the order my brain thought fit.

'These clothes!' I breathed, without pausing in my self-imposed task of trying to induce order into the chaos.

'I know.' Caroline looked at them dismissively, 'A load of old rubbish, really.'

'Old *rubbish*? My God, if you found any of these in a vintage shop in Singapore . . .' I pulled out a pale blue, satin coat trimmed with ribbon. It was next to an orange suit, totally in the wrong place. 'This is fantastic. But not perhaps positioned here,' I said, moving it further down the hanging rail.

'You like it?' asked Caroline in surprise. 'Have it.'

'I couldn't!'

'My dear girl, I don't want it.'

'But surely the sentimental value . . . I mean, your memories—'

'My memories are in here,' she tapped her head. 'Not in there.' She surveyed the melee of clothes, then picked up a small piece of bone on a leather cord. 'Now, *this* I'm rather fond of.'

'That?' I tried to summon some enthusiasm. 'Well, it's—'

'It was given to me by my first husband. It's a deer's antler, the first stag he ever shot. Have you ever shot a deer, my dear?'

'Erm . . . no. I can't say I have. We don't get many stags in Singapore. But it's very nice,' I lied, so pinched myself in self-rebuke.

'And this little lovely,' she picked up an embroidered purse. 'I bought this at a street market in Nepal. Bartered for it with my last packet of cigarettes before we trekked to the basecamp at on the Everest. Have you been to Nepal?'

'No, not there either,' I said, feeling rather inadequate. God, I felt under travelled. I scrabbled around in my mind, trying to think of somewhere I had been that would impress her—but, come to think of it, I realized it was a paltry line-up. Malaysia and Batam, that was about it. Oh, and Sentosa Island. Why hadn't I been anywhere exciting? Why hadn't I trekked around Nepal?

'I haven't really travelled much at all,' I admitted reluctantly.

'Well, you must, dear girl!' boomed Caroline. 'You must broaden your horizons. Learn about life from real people. One of the dearest friends I have in the world is a nun from a convent in Bolivia. We ground coffee together in the mountains.'

'Wow.'

A little clock on the mantelpiece chimed the half hour, and I suddenly realized that we were not getting anywhere.

'So anyway . . . did you have any ideas for a wedding outfit?'

'Something warm and colourful,' said Caroline, reaching for a thick, red-and-yellow poncho.

'Erm . . . I'm not so sure that that would be entirely appropriate . . .' I pushed between the jackets and dresses, and suddenly espied a flash of apricot silk. 'Ooh! This is nice.' I haul it out—and I couldn't believe my eyes. It was Balenciaga.

'My going-away outfit,' said Caroline reminiscently. 'We travelled on the Orient Express to Venice and then explored the caves of Postojna. Do you know that region?'

'You have to wear this!' I squeaked in excitement. 'You'll look spectacular. And it's so romantic, wearing your own going-away outfit!'

'I suppose it might be rather fun.' She held it up against herself with red, weather-beaten hands that made me wince just to look at them. 'That should still fit, shouldn't it? Now, there must be a hat around here somewhere . . .' She put down the suit and started rummaging around on a shelf.

It took me a while to persuade Caroline out of the green, felt hat and into a chic, black cloche.

'Thank you, dear,' said Caroline.

'You're welcome,' I smiled.

As I turned to leave, she said, 'Make sure you're happy. Never compromise on that, my dear.'

'Sorry?' I wasn't quite following her train of thought.

'I can see you're special. You have your own way about you. I notice things, you see. But, Clara, never allow anyone to make you feel sad or undervalued. Promise me?'

'I promise,' I replied, 'and thank you.'

'Okay, off you go, then,' Caroline hustled me from the room.

As I walked back along the corridor towards Jenny's room, I heard some familiar voices in the hall downstairs.

'It's common knowledge, foot-and-mouth was caused by carrier pigeons.'

'Pigeons? You're telling me that this huge epidemic, which wiped out stocks of cattle across Europe, was caused by a few harmless pigeons?'

'Harmless? Jack, they're vermin!'

I hurried to the balustrade—and there they were, standing by the fireplace, Jenny's father, Clive, and Jack. Both were in morning dress suits with a top hat each under their arms and Maureen appeared beside them, dressed in a navy jacket, floral skirt and bright red shoes that didn't quite match her red hat.

I decided to go down and meet them.

'Clara, is Nicholas with you?' asked Maureen looking around with bright eyes, like a squirrel searching for a nut.

'He's somewhere around,' I said.

Nicholas eventually showed up along with John and Mike.

'Where have you three terrors been?' demanded Maureen .

'A few games of pool, Mum,' Mike replied.

'Yes and a few glasses of whisky too, by the smell of it. I think you two best go and get yourselves cleaned up. Look at your brother, he's ready.'

Caroline joined us and I was pleased to see that she was in the outfit I had selected.

In the distance, I could hear the church bells ringing, and there was a kind of excited, expectant atmosphere in the air. Jenny's father, who was still talking to Jack, turned to me and asked, 'And where's the blushing bride?'

'I'm here,' came Jenny's voice. We all looked up—and there she was, floating down the stairs, clutching a stunning bouquet of white roses and ivy.

'Oh, Jenny,' sighed Caroline and clapped a hand to her mouth. 'Oh, that dress! Oh . . . Jenny! You're going to look—' She turned to me with softened eyes and for the first time seemed to take in my dress. 'Clara . . . is that what you're wearing? You'll freeze!'

'No, I won't. The church is going to be heated, I'm sure.' I fervently hoped it was.

'I wouldn't count on it,' Nicholas chimed in.

'It'll be your turn soon, Clara,' said Jenny.

'Sorry? My turn?' I asked.

'To get married.'

'Did you get that, Nicholas?' asked Jack with a wide grin.

'Oh . . . Clara has a good ten years before she need worry about anything like that . . .' said Nicholas, conversationally.

'What?' Maureen stiffened, her eyes darting from Nicholas to me and back again. 'What did you say?'

'Clara wants to wait at least ten years before she gets married,' said Nicholas. 'Isn't that right, Clara?' There was a stunned silence. I could feel my face growing hot.

'Um . . .' I cleared my throat and strived for a nonchalant smile. 'That's . . . that's right. I want to focus on my career. Why is that such a surprise? It's not like anyone has proposed.'

'Really?' exclaimed Jenny, staring at me, wide-eyed. 'I didn't know that! Why?'

'So I can . . . um . . . explore my full potential,' I mumbled, not daring to look at Maureen. 'And . . . get to know the real me.'

'Get to know the real you?' Maureen's voice was slightly shrill. 'Why do you need ten years to do that? I could show it to you in ten minutes!'

'But Clara, how old will you be in ten years' time?' asked Jenny, wrinkling her brow.

'I won't necessarily need ten whole years exactly,' I said, starting to feel a little rattled. 'You know, maybe . . . eight will be long enough. Or . . . just a week. It's not really up to me, is it?'

Somewhere deep down, I hoped, of course, that someone would one day propose to me, and that someone, I hoped, would be Nicholas. But I didn't want to sound desperate. The ten-year wait was just a passing comment, me not wanting to sound easy.

'Nicholas,' said Jenny, looking mischievous. 'The window of opportunity is open it seems. You should snap her up.' I blushed and thought that was really sweet of her to say so.

'I will take it under consideration,' said Nicholas, which wasn't the most romantic thing to have said. Then as if on cue, Sprout appeared and started to hump his leg.

Thankfully Jenny took the spotlight off us at that moment and almost shrieked, 'Five minutes and then we have to leave?'

'Yes, I too must get ready,' I made my escape. I was cross. When I wanted to get married was my decision. Yes, okay, I was obsessed with finding a man, but getting married was serious stuff. Why did I suddenly feel like a horse being auctioned off at a market for breeding? I came on this trip to meet his family, not to be vetted as potential wife and mother material. I needed to talk to Nicholas about this . . .

But maybe this was just the way people got at weddings, all maudlin and sentimental.

Chapter 20

By the time, I had found my shoes, redone my lipstick and come downstairs, only Nicholas was left in the hall.

'My parents have gone over,' he said. 'Jenny says we should go over too, and she'll come with her father in the carriage. Also, I've found a coat for you,' he added, offering a sheepskin jacket.

'I'm fine for now, thanks. Maybe later.' A decision I was sure to regret later, as my simple, black dress was made for the tropics, not the biting cold of the highlands.

'Okay,' he said, 'but I will bring it along in case you need it later.'

As Nicholas and I made our way over the gravel to the tented walkway, the air was still and silent and a watery sun emerged. The pealing bells had diminished to single chimes, and there was no one about except a solitary, scurrying waiter. Everyone else was probably already inside.

'Sorry if I brought up a sensitive subject just then,' said Nicholas, as we began to walk towards the church.

'Sensitive?' I raised my eyebrows. 'Oh, what, *that*. That's not a sensitive subject at all.'

'I see. So, you're open to a proposal then?' he asked. My God, did he just give me a hint? I felt myself teetering on the edge of a panic attack and I groped instinctively for my rubber band.

'Absolutely,' I nodded. 'Any time.' In the distance, I could hear the crunch of hooves on gravel, which was probably Jenny's carriage setting off. 'Or you know, maybe I can wait,' I tagged on casually. 'Or . . . maybe not, just go with the heart.' I felt myself wanting to shut up.

The long silence was only broken by the soft, rhythmic sound of our footsteps on the walkway. The atmosphere had grown very strained between us, and I didn't dare look at Nicholas. I cleared my throat, rubbed my nose and tried to think of a something neutral to say, a comment about the weather perhaps.

We reached the church's gate and Nicholas turned to me—his face stripped of its customary quizzical expression.

'Seriously, Clara,' he said, 'are you open to getting married?'

'I . . . yes, I am,' I said and smiled.

In the moment of stillness between us, my heart started to thump really hard. Oh, my God. Oh, my God. Maybe he was going to . . . maybe he was about to—'

'Ah! Last-minute guests!' The vicar bustled out of the porch and both Nicholas and I jumped. 'All set for the wedding?' he asked.

'I, er . . . think so,' I said, aware of Nicholas still looking at me.

'Yes, we are,' I said. Hoping he meant Jenny and Gilbert, not our own.

'Good. You'd better get inside!' exclaimed the vicar. 'You don't want to miss the moment!'

'No,' said Nicholas, after a pause. 'No, we don't.' He dropped a kiss on my shoulder and walked in without saying anything else, and I stared after him, baffled.

Did we just talk about . . . was Nicholas about to . . .

The sound of hooves jolted me out of my reverie. I turned to see Jenny's carriage bowling down the road like something straight out of a fairy tale. Her veil was blowing in the wind and she was smiling radiantly at the people who had stopped to watch.

We entered the church—and there was Gilbert, waiting with his best man. He was as tall and skinny as ever, and his face still reminded me of a stoat, but I had to admit he looked pretty striking in his sporran and kilt. He gazed at Jenny with such transparent love and admiration that I could feel my nose start to prickle. He turned briefly to her, met her eye and grinned nervously—and she smiled back shyly.

The vicar began his 'dearly beloved' speech, and I felt myself beam with pleasure. I planned to relish every single, familiar word. This was like watching the start of a favourite movie, with Jenny and Gilbert playing the lead.

'Jenny, wilt thou take this man to be thy lawfully wedded husband?' The vicar had a huge bushy beard, which seemed to rise at every question, almost as though he were afraid the answer might be 'no'. 'Wilt thou love him, comfort him, honour and keep him in sickness and in health; and, forsaking all others, keep thee only unto him, so long as ye both shall live?'

There was a pause—then, in a voice as clear as a bell, Jenny said, 'I will.'

When it came to the bit where Jenny and Gilbert must hold hands, Jenny passed her bouquet to her maid of honour. I took the opportunity to turn around and take a quick peek at the congregation. The place was packed to the rafters, in fact there wasn't even room for everyone to sit down. There were lots of strapping men in kilts and women in velvet suits, and then, there was a whole crowd of their London friends standing at the back of the tiny church. And there was Maureen squashed right up against Jack, with a tissue pressed to her eyes and bookended by Mike and John. Sally was standing behind her. She looked up and saw me and I gave a little smile. She smiled back.

I turned back to find that Jenny and Gilbert were now kneeling side by side as the vicar intoned severely, 'Those whom God hath joined together, let no man put asunder.'

I looked at Jenny as she smiled at Gilbert. She was completely lost in him. Jenny and Gilbert belonged to each other now. I suddenly feel slightly sad. I wanted to be married, too.

I watched as the vicar placed his hand on Jenny's and Gilbert's heads to bless them—and felt a tiny tear begin to form in the corner of my eye. I looked over at Nicholas and smiled tremulously. He was too mesmerized by the ceremony to be aware that I was looking at him.

Suddenly I felt in need of a little reassurance. I quickly scanned the rows of guests, looking for my own mother. For a few moments there, I actually believed she was here and although I bravely held my confident smile, I felt a ridiculous panic rise inside me, like a child realizing she had been left behind at school; that everyone else had been collected but me. I remembered that Nicholas was right there beside me, so what possible harm could I come to? The momentary twinge of anxiety dissipated as quickly as it had reared its head. I felt calm again.

Nicholas was looking directly at me and no one else. And, as I gazed back at him, I felt restored. I had been collected, too; it was all okay.

Later, as we emerged into the churchyard, Nicholas was swept away from me by a flood of bodies, just as the bells pealed thunderously overhead. The crowd which had gathered outside on the road set up a cheer.

'Congratulations!' I cried, giving Jenny a huge hug. 'And to you, Gilbert!' Confetti filled the air engulfing us like a sudden snow storm. Guests were already piling out of the church in droves, talking and laughing and calling to each other in loud confident voices. They swarmed around Jenny and Gilbert, kissing and hugging and shaking hands, and I moved away a little, wondering where Nicholas was.

'Here. Put this on,' Nicholas's voice was suddenly in my ear, and I turned around to see him, along with the rest of his family. He was holding out his jacket. 'You must be freezing, Clara. Put this on.'

'Don't worry. I'm fine!' I replied bravely. I was actually freezing but didn't want to make a fuss.

'No. You're not fine. Your body is not used to this weather,' he stated more firmly. He had a point. This was a far cry from Singapore.

'Clara, do as you are told, my girl. There may not be snow on the ground, but it's brass monkeys out here.' Jack stepped forward, took the jacket from Nicholas and draped it around my shoulders.

'Very nice wedding,' he added.

'Yes,' I replied and then glanced at Nicholas wondering if, by any chance, we could work the conversation back to what we were talking about right before the service. But Nicholas was looking at Jenny and Gilbert, who were being photographed under a tree. Jenny looked rapturous, but Gilbert looked like he was facing a firing squad.

'He's a very nice bloke,' said Jack, nodding towards Gilbert. 'A bit odd though, but all right.'

'Yes. He is, Jack,' I had to agree.

'Would you like a glass of hot Scottish whisky?' interrupted a waiter, coming up with a tray. 'Or champagne?'

'Ooh, hot whisky,' I said gratefully. 'Thanks.' I took a few sips and closed my eyes as the warmth spread through my body. If only it could get down to my feet, which, to be honest, were completely frozen.

'Bridesmaids!' cried Jenny suddenly. 'Where's Clara? We need you for a photograph!'

My eyes snapped opened. 'Here,' I shouted. I handed Nicholas his jacket back and my drink and hurried through the gaggle of women and joined Jenny and Gilbert. I didn't feel cold any more. I smiled my most radiant smile, held aloft the bunch of flowers that I had just been given to me, linked arms with Jenny when the photographer told me to and in between shots, waved at Maureen and Jack, who had pushed their way to the front of the crowd.

'We'll head back to the house soon,' said Caroline, coming up to kiss Jenny. 'People are getting chilly. It rather feels like Scotland. You can finish the pictures there.'

'Okay,' said Jenny. 'But let's just take some of Clara and me. I'm not sure when I will see you again,' she held my hand.

'Good idea!' agreed Gilbert at once and headed off in obvious relief to talk to his father, who looked exactly like Gilbert but forty years older. The photographer took a few shots of Jenny and me beaming at each other and then paused to reload his camera. Jenny accepted a glass of whisky from a waiter.

'Don't worry, this is for Gilbert. I've stopped drinking,' she said. I was happy about that. 'Clara, listen,' she whispered in my ear and I turned to find her gazing at me earnestly; she was so close, I could almost count the peach fuzz on her face, 'I need to ask you something. Would you really marry now if Nicholas asked you?'

'Yes, I would,' I admitted, not really sure why she would ask me that question, especially on her own wedding day. I could see in her face, by her pensive expression that she had another question about to burst from her lips. 'And d'you think Nicholas could be the one? Just between us girls.'

I took a long pause, thinking about it. We did get along. We had a strong chemistry and we laughed at the same things, but most of all, when we were apart, at least for me, I felt like a part of me was missing.

'Yes, very much so,' I said confidently, feeling a deep pink flood my cheeks. 'Yes. I think he is.' Jenny looked searchingly at me for a few moments longer—then abruptly seemed to come to a decision. 'Right!' she said, putting down the whisky, 'I'm going to throw my bouquet.'

'What?' I stared at her in bewilderment. 'Jenny, don't be silly. You can't throw your bouquet yet!'

'Yes, I can! I can throw it whenever I like.'

'You should throw it just before you leave for your honeymoon!'

'I don't care,' said Jenny obstinately. 'I can't wait any longer. I'm going to throw it now.'

'But you're supposed to do it at the *end*!' I protested.

'Who's the bride? You or me? If I wait till the end, it won't be any fun! Now, stand over there,' she waved me away, 'and put your bag down. You'll never catch it if you're holding things! Ladies!' she raised her voice, 'I'm going to throw my bouquet now, okay?'

'Okay,' Gilbert called out cheerfully. 'Good idea.'

'Go on, Jenny!' I heard Mike shout.

'Honestly! I don't even want to catch it!' I said.

'Come on, Clara.' Sally was now pulling me into the gathering group of young ladies.

I supposed that I should try because I was asked by the bride, no less, to join in. Most of the women around me were bridesmaids—so I decided to go along and respect the invitation.

'I want a picture of this,' Nicholas was saying to the photographer. 'And where's Gilbert?'

The slightly weird thing was the bridesmaids suddenly melted away and there was no one vying for the bouquet with me. I noticed Gilbert and his best man going around, murmuring in people's ears and gradually all the guests turned to me with bright, expectant faces.

'Ready?' called Jenny.

'Wait!' I cried. 'You haven't got enough people yet! There should be lots of us.'

I felt so stupid to be among these women. I didn't really have any right. Honestly, I should have just stepped aside.

'Wait!' I cried, but it was too late.

'Catch!' Jenny yelled. 'Catch!'

The bouquet came looping through the air in an arc, and I needed to jump up slightly to catch it. It was bigger and heavier than I had expected and for a moment, I just stared at it, secretly half-delighted and half completely furious with myself for even going for it. Then everyone gathered around me and I was handed a tiny envelope by Sally. It was addressed to me: '*To Clara.*'

An envelope addressed to me? Why would I be given an envelope at someone's wedding in a foreign country that I had never been to before. I look up bewildered at Nicholas who, with a shining face, nodded towards the envelope. He gestured to me to open it.

Mike and John took a break from flirting with the single bridesmaids and teasing Nicholas for being so prim and proper to come and see what was going on.

'Go on open it,' said John. 'It's okay, Clara, you can.' Sally said.

With trembling fingers, I opened the envelope. There was something lumpy inside. It was . . .

It was a ring, all wrapped up in cotton wool. I took it out, feeling dizzy. There was a message on the card, written in Nicholas's handwriting. It said: '*Will You . . .*'

I stared in disbelief, keeping an iron rein on my self-control but the world started to spin around, and the blood thundered in my head. I looked up at Nicholas, his eyes were smiling and warm.

'Clara—' he began, and there was a tiny intake of breath around the churchyard 'Will you—' It was then that I realized what he is about to do. My world stopped as a million and one thoughts exploded in my head. Wasn't this what I had wanted all along? So, why was I so scared? From the moment I laid eyes on him, I knew there was something special between us. Again, I began to question what I wanted.

Clara, get a grip, I screamed inside my own head. He was perfect for me and I truly believed that we loved each other. Did I? Love him . . . *oh God, what should I do?* Everyone was looking at me.

I turned around on the spot, my eyes closed and willed my heart to make the decision for me.

'Yes! Yeee-esssss!' I heard myself declare and then a joyful applause erupted through the churchyard before I even realized that I had spoken. I was so charged with emotion, that my voice didn't even *sound* like mine. In fact, I sounded more like . . . Maureen. I couldn't believe it. As I whipped round, she clapped a hand over her mouth in embarrassment.

'Sorry!' she whispered, and a ripple of laughter ran through the group of people gathered around me.

Nicholas looked at me. 'Clara, if I had to wait five years, then I would. Or eight—or even ten.' He paused. 'Maybe not ten.' He paused again and there was complete silence, 'But I hope that one day—preferably sooner rather than that—you'll do me the honour of marrying me.'

My throat was so tight, I couldn't speak. I gave a tiny nod, and Nicholas took my hand in his. He unfolded my fingers, took the ring and slid it on to my finger. My heart thudded. Nicholas wanted me to marry him. He must have been planning this all along, without saying a thing. That was why he wanted to bring me here on this trip to meet his family.

I went dewy-eyed just looking at the ring. It was a diamond ring. It was perfect. He looked at me, his eyes more tender than I had ever seen them and he kissed me, and then the cheering started.

I couldn't believe it. I was engaged and I couldn't wait to tell my mother.

Chapter 21

Six wonderful months had passed since my engagement to Nicholas. Loretta, Ken, Tony Chan, Pauline Chan and, of course, my mother were over the moon when they discovered that I was engaged to be married. I hadn't been back for more than a few days before my mother and the others started to help me plan the wedding.

Life had been perfect, in fact. Nicholas and I had become even closer as a couple, and I could even put up with his breaking wind in bed now. But perhaps not everyone was happy. Jared congratulated us by saying that he was delighted for us, but his curt and standoffish behaviour from that point onwards seemed to indicate otherwise.

Despite that, we did, as a team, manage to put in place some ideas that Nicholas and I had gained from our time in London. We had selected a few ideas from each of the hotels we had visited and studied; and then coupled them with Nicholas's marketing ideas. They had all begun to bear fruit and Tony was delighted. New cocktails in the bar, with names like the Duxton Sling, Indulgence, and the Ring of Fire were launched. They proved to be so popular the hotel bar in itself was making a profit. On Friday evenings the bar was jam packed. We added a touch of flair and comfort to the lobby and general seating areas with deep red and purple velvet chairs, and rich, Egyptian, high-thread-count sheets in every bedroom, set upon the most comfortable mattresses you could find. Perfection was applied to anything and everything that ensured our guests comfort and needs. But above all, the Duxton Heritage had a new identity, in that it screamed class, originality and uniqueness. Fresh coats of paint and tile were applied to lift the freshness of every surface.

Life was going so well and everything was working out splendidly, but the happiness that I had been feeling just ended. My dearest, sweetest Pauline died on this day. Or, maybe, it was the previous day. I couldn't be sure in all honesty as it was all so sudden and shocking. My mind was in a state of disbelief. Pauline was family to me, and her loss was hard to bear.

Mr Chan personally called me to break the sad news. In his own dear words he described what had transpired: they had been spending a few weeks at their home on the main island. They loved Hong Kong in so many ways, not least because it was where they had made their fortune with their very first hotel. It had also become their home away from home. Pauline had especially loved looking at the harbour and the endless crossing of the White Star ferry against the vista of Kowloon at sunset—it always brought her peace and contentment was what she used to say.

That morning, however, Tony had woken up to not find her sleeping restfully beside him as he had done for the past forty years. He was, understandably, concerned. I couldn't even begin to imagine what it must have felt like when he had found his dear, cherished wife, his soul mate, in the early hours of that morning, sitting motionless in her favourite armchair by the window overlooking the harbour.

The doctor had come and pronounced her dead. She had simply passed away from natural causes. At least that was what the death certificate had noted. The wake and funeral, he told me, would be a small, private affair. It was all planned to take place on the day after tomorrow which just coincidentally happened to be my wedding day.

I felt upset that there was just enough time to book a flight from Singapore to Hong Kong and make the wake. But Tony specifically told me to remain at the hotel to help the staff during this difficult time. Not to mention my special day.

Without the Chans, I felt a deep sadness and a void within my soul.

I could imagine Pauline lying there in her silk-lined casket. Her sweet face, even in death, looking as if she were about to break into a smile. The guest list would be, as Tony described it, very small. Oh, how I wished I were there.

But wait, what was I talking about, I would be there. I would be there in spirit and say my goodbyes. May God bless you, Pauline. We will watch over Mr Chan for you, until you both reunite in the great beyond.

I had so wanted her to be at my wedding. It would have made the day even more special. I would think of her on the day. She would never be forgotten; I would make sure of that. Weeks of planning had taken place and she had helped me. And now she wouldn't be there. She had given me strict instructions about what to wear and say. I would always remember her wise words: 'It is your day and your day alone.'

I hoped Pauline had liked Nicholas. I had never had a chance to ask her. Oh, no! What if she felt that I was doing the wrong thing? Perhaps she will send me a sign—a door would slam or a zephyr would blow the veil off my head. In her own way, Pauline would let me know. I closed my eyes and prayed that Pauline could hear me. Was I mad to even think such a thing?

I pulled myself together. This day was not about me. It was about remembering Pauline, a dear, sweet lady. It was difficult but I had to get a grip. We were to fly out to London the following day for my wedding. I couldn't be a blubbering wreck, could I? Pauline wouldn't want that.

Picturing the charming allure of the church and remembering the sound of the church bells ringing, soothed my heart a little—and I consoled myself with the fact that life must go on.

Chapter 22

In the lull before the storm—in this case, the blessed quiet before the bridal suite was overrun by the wedding party—Loretta stared critically down at a freshly painted, blood-red fingernail and said, 'This isn't right. It needs to be subtle. I don't want to be a bridesmaid at a vampire wedding.' She glanced across the room at me and smiled widely. 'I bet you expected me to be *impossible*. Freaking out by now didn't you?' It was a statement that was so perfectly dropped in the moment that I wanted it imprinted into my memory forever.

'It should be more petal-pink than blood-red, don't you think?' I heard Loretta tell the nail lady. She nodded towards the pearl-pink bridesmaid's dress that hung from a satin hanger on the outside of a wardrobe. 'You don't want to look like countess Dracula.' Loretta met my eyes again, this time with a roll of her eyes at the make-up artist's ineptitude.

Just as I made it into the Rolls Royce, my phone text alert chirped into life. I wasn't prepared for the disaster to unfold.

JOHN: HI, IT'S JOHN. I'M WITH MIKE AT HEATHROW TO COLLECT YOUR MOTHER BUT SHE NEVER APPEARED. HEADING BACK NOW AND WILL TRY AND MEET YOU AT THE CHURCH.

Anxiety inundated my entire being. Maureen, being the bloodhound that she was, noticed. I hadn't had such an attack in ages.

'I have to call my mum. Now!' I shrieked.

'Whatever is the matter, dear?' Maureen asked.

I handed her the phone. 'That was John. He's with Mike. Mum never showed up.' I felt like I was about to faint.

'Okay. Calm down, dear. Let me call her for you now.'

I fumbled with the phone, found Mum's number and then handed the phone back to Maureen. My entire world felt as if it had just plunged into an abyss.

Maureen extricated herself from the car and on to the grass verge. I could see her on the phone, pacing back and forth like a caged tiger.

I wished I could call Nicholas. I really needed him now. But then, I was sure John and Mike had already done that. So, there I was, sat in the rear of a Rolls Royce in my designer wedding dress, on a perfect English summer's day, ready to marry the man of my dreams and my own mother had gone missing.

Maureen appeared at the open door of the car. 'Not coming, dear. She's still in Singapore. She missed the flight and says she is really sorry. So, here is what we're going to do.' Maureen had already decided on a plan, which was good in a way. But now, I was trying to process the fact that Mum had missed the flight. How could she have done so? I should have had Ken or Loretta bring her over. How stupid I had been to think my mum, who had never left the shores of Singapore, could have boarded a flight to the UK on her own.

'Sorry, what now?' I asked.

'We carry on, dear. Get you to the church. We will have another wedding in Singapore just for your mum, okay?' She made it all sound so simple.

I should have brought Mum with me . . . this was all my fault. I felt the urge to twang, but no rubber band. Nonetheless, I started to twang, until a firm hand gripped my wrist.

'It'll all be fine,' assured Maureen. 'Let's go,' she ordered the driver and we set off before I had a chance to worry further.

A while later, the door of the Rolls Royce opened to reveal a sea of people gathered around the portico of the church. But something was wrong. I could sense it. They were too quiet. Not that I was expecting a movie-star welcome or anything; but smiling faces at the very least. I looked at their faces again. Yes, something was definitely wrong; their faces were etched with concern.

'Something's wrong,' I said out loud. Maureen had realized it, too.

'There, there, dear. I'll go and see.' She alighted first and strode purposefully towards them. Meanwhile I slid out and waited for her by the car. Jack appeared beside me and took my hand in his.

'Hi, darling,' he said, calmly. It was then that I noticed his expression. You know, the kind of expression people have when they want to tell you something that they know you wouldn't want to hear. A sort of a pained expression.

'Jack,' I said, studying his face. 'is everything okay?' I asked nervously. Sally then appeared, and then I knew. She too looked concerned. 'Will someone please tell me what's happened?' I repeated.

'Well, it's like this, dear,' he replied. His voice sounded hoarse and he continued, 'The vicar has fallen sick. Case of the flu, I'm told, so . . .'

When you drew the curtains closed at night, what little remained of the daylight would fade slowly until everything went pitch black. That was what I just experienced, only I had fainted.

The first I knew of this was being slapped gently across the face by Maureen. I was on the grass and Maureen's worried face slowly came into view. Then Sally's.

'Clara. Clara, my dear. You fainted,' she said.

'What?' was all I could manage. I blinked a few times to bring myself back to full consciousness.

'Nicholas is here,' said Sally. Nicholas then appeared, leaning over me.

'Clara. Don't worry; we can get married another day.' By now I was struggling to get a grip. Did he just suggest that our wedding be postponed? I tried processing it all for a moment. First, my mum doesn't show up, then the vicar is ill. Right! All perfectly normal. Someone please tell me that this is not happening.

I was given a glass of water. I had no idea why. But why was it, whenever people fainted, they were given water to drink? Nonetheless, as I was sweating like a pig because of the sudden hot flush, the cold glass of water was most welcome. It was a simple case of my anxiety getting the better of me. And no, I hadn't fainted because I was pregnant or had the flu.

Nicholas sat beside me on the grass outside the church and smiled sweetly. 'We could look at it in a positive way. We can reschedule and your mum can come,' he said.

'I guess you're right,' I said with a weak chuckle.

Loretta appeared beside me in her bridesmaid's dress. For once she said nothing and just smiled, which I assumed was her just being happy for me.

'Well, that just puts the icing on the bloody cake!' I heard Jack shouting at someone.

'Dad, what's happened?' Nicholas jumped to his feet.

'The bloody catering firm has gone bust, so no food now.'

It felt like everyone turned to me. 'Well,' I shrugged, weakly, 'they say things go wrong in threes.'

'I could get the girls together and knock up a feast?' said Maureen, undaunted.

'Not much point, Mum, without us being married,' Nicholas gently placated her.

'Come on, everyone, back to Downe Hall. Let's get pissed,' Jack announced.

'Good idea, Dad, let's do that.' Mike was never one to turn down an opportunity to have a drink.

With what looked like perfect timing, John came running up, 'Did I miss anything?'

'Yes, as always,' said Mike sarcastically.

We all looked at John and burst out laughing, and then headed off back to Downe Hall.

* * *

The wedding was a catastrophe for obvious reasons. We cancelled the enormous after-party that was going to be held at Downe Hall late into the night. We fed and provided drinks for those who felt the need to join and console us. Upon reflection, we should have just had our wedding in Singapore and not have agreed to all this fuss. But the past is now the past, and the future beckons.

Nicholas and I retired early to our room to prepare ourselves, both mentally and physically, to fly back to Singapore. At least that was the intent. Instead, we collapsed, exhausted and drained, into bed. Both of us were still trying to fathom what had just happened. The simple truth was: our wedding didn't happen. A statement of fact and nothing we could have done would have made any difference. Maybe we should have just counted it as a blessing of some kind. Life, obviously, had other plans for us. That question could be tackled in the morning. For the moment, we both needed to close our eyes.

Chapter 23

Both Nicholas and I cast ourselves wholeheartedly into work, almost as soon as the wheels of our plane touched down at Changi airport in Singapore. It was so good to be home. Our phones sprang to life the second we turned them on and we started to digest the never-ending streams of messages regarding our failed wedding. We needed to take our minds off the wedding-that-wasn't somehow. That said, fourteen hours locked in a plane together had afforded us the chance to talk. We were both okay. As in, really okay. Not a twang of my rubber band in fourteen hours. The failed wedding didn't negate or reduce the feelings we had for each other, in fact, I felt even closer to him now. We agreed to simply set another date. We also agreed, and I was secretly happy about it, that the wedding would be held in Singapore. We left the airport, refreshed, optimistic and blissfully happy. What could possibly go wrong now?

We wasted no time in setting up a meeting with Jared and taking him through our strategy to launch the new and improved Duxton Heritage brand. Despite the non-wedding, during our trip to London, we had at least scouted out some competition. As it turned out, I had a flair for marketing and absorbed ideas like a sponge from floral displays to Michelin-star menus to web-site designs and I added my own Singapore flavour to everything we observed and angled it back to the Duxton. Of course, Nicholas helped by dragging me out of rabbit holes if I strayed off track. Jared seemed almost dumbstruck, but he loved the ideas we had generated. Within a few short weeks, bookings had gone through the roof, and we hadn't even started the structural renovations yet.

Nicholas said my strategy was brilliant, which I guess it was in some way. It had worked. Not that I thought my ideas and suggestions were all that special—just obvious changes. I mean, you just had to state the obvious, right? The Duxton had history, it had charm and when you infused that with what was relevant today, you got something that was unique. You don't sell people a product, you sell them what they want or need, and uniqueness seemed to sell. So, that was what the Duxton became—a unique, boutique, heritage hotel.

Normality soon became the new normal over the next few weeks and I arrived for work as I always did on a Friday morning, on time.

I was summoned an hour or so later to Mr Chan's office to discuss what I thought was a change in the restaurant's menu. It turned out to be something very different.

I simply didn't expect what happened to happen. There I was, seated, in front of his desk, listening to his words, but I simply couldn't process them. Not much of a revelation considering I wasn't the sharpest tool in the box at the best of times.

'Are you even listening to me, my dear?' Mr Chan asked again. He repeated the very words that had just reduced me to a blubbering, emotional wreck.

'I'm sorry. Can you repeat that again, please?' I asked.

'Yes, of course. I have decided to retire. So, in the absence of any children or grandchildren, I'm leaving the entire hotel chain to you, Clara.' He waited for a sign—any sign—to show his words had sunk in.

'Yes. That's what I thought you said,' I muttered, still unable to believe it.

'Well? Do you accept?' Mr Chan repeated the question like he had asked for something as mundane as whether I would buy him a coffee.

'But why? Why me?' I realized I had just asked him two questions, both as lame as the other.

'It's what Pauline and I always planned. You were in our minds as our daughter. Family. You helped save the chain. I couldn't think of a better and safer pair of hands.' He rose, walked around the table, bent down and hugged me.

'I won't take no for an answer. But, if you want to sell it all, you can. Do whatever you wish. Just as I will now do,' he smiled.

'I don't know what to say,' I replied, which hardly seemed adequate. I hugged him tightly.

'Okay, my dear. Don't break me in two.' I let him go and he perched on the edge of the table.

'I must tell Nicholas; we're to be married. Well, we've agreed to try again. Loretta, I should tell her. And my mother. Oh, my God, I have to tell everyone,' I paused. 'Is that all right? I mean, can I, before I faint?' I asked.

Mr Chan placed a gentle hand on my shoulder, 'Take a breath, my dear,' he said calmly, 'you can tell the world, if you like. I will arrange for a press release, too.'

And then it happened again. Those night curtains closed in on me. My world turned pitch black. The next thing I knew, I was surrounded by people. I was looking directly up at them. Loretta was fanning me with a sheaf of papers, kneeling by my side. Their faces, blurry at first, slowly came into focus.

'What happened?' I asked, trying to sit up.

'Easy, babe. You fainted. Mr Chan here managed to catch you. It's okay.' I looked around and saw Mr Chan's sweet face among the faces peering anxiously at me.

'Drink this, dear,' he handed me a glass of water and I sipped it.

'So, now that you're a millionaire hotelier, I guess I should start calling you "the boss",' Loretta joked.

'You told them?' I asked.

'Well, I had to explain why you fainted,' he said, at which everyone laughed. It was as if the entire hotel's staff was in the room. To me, they were family.

'I think we had best plan that wedding again. Can't have you running this place all on your own.' To my astonishment, Nicholas shouldered through crowd and placed his arm around my shoulders. I, of course, smiled. 'Tony wanted me here to witness the breaking news.'

'I'm not alone. I have everyone here,' I started to cry again.

'It's okay. You're in shock, Clara. Now let's give her some air, shall we?' Ken announced, handing me a clean napkin to wipe my tear-stained face.

'Clara Tan, will you, for the second time, marry me?' asked Nicholas smiling. Before I could open my mouth to reply, the entire room erupted in a wild cheering.

'Champagne all round! This really is the time to celebrate,' announced Mr Chan.

'May I?' I shouted rather loudly and the room fell silent. 'Thank you. Today I've been shown that by two people. I owe them both so much. Thank you, Mr Chan. I will make you proud and never allow this place to be sold. As, for you, Nicholas Tate, yes, I will marry you.'

After that, the room burst into cacophony again and nothing was going to stop us all from having fun.

* * *

It was gone midnight by the time I reached home. My mother was sat in front of the TV, a glass of warm milk clasped in her hands. She was watching a late-night documentary on crimes in Singapore. It was something that fascinated her.

'Hi, Mum,' I kissed her on the forehead. Her eyes remained rivetted to the TV screen.

'How was your day, dear?' she asked.

'Oh, you know, very typical, Mum.'

'Oh, that's good, dear.'

'Something happened, Mum, something amazing.'

'What was that?'

'Mr Chan just made me a millionaire and Nicholas proposed to me again.'

'That's nice, dear.' Mothers. What was one to do? But at least she was happy too.

'Don't stay up too late, Mum. I'm off to bed, good night.' I leave her be and went to my room, still smiling.

'Clara,' she called.

'Yes mum, what is it?'

She appeared at my bedroom doorway. 'I'm happy for you, really I am. I just don't want to lose you, like I did your father,' she said. I was shocked. It struck me, at that very moment, that she had been carrying this guilt for all these years.

She continued, 'I didn't miss the plane to London, I stood at the gate for an hour, thinking about stepping on board, until it was too late, and the plane left without me. I'm so sorry, Clara.' Tears streamed down her face.

'Mum, it's okay,' I got up and hugged her. 'What's wrong?' I asked.

'I never want you to suffer the loss of a husband like I did, so I couldn't bare to witness your getting married,' her embrace got tighter.

'It wasn't your fault, Mum. He left because he was weak, and you have been strong.'

'But your OCD, it's because of his leaving,' she wept.

'No, Mum, my OCD is just life's gift.' That moment was special as my mum, and I finally let go of the ghosts of the past. It was a wonderful feeling. Tomorrow would be a whole new day and plans would have to be made. I would wake up a hotelier.

Chapter 24

I couldn't believe I had made it to this moment. I honestly couldn't believe it was really happening to me. I felt like I had been on a roller coaster for the past few months, and I wasn't talking about the press conference last week that announced to the world that little old me, Clara Tan, from my humble beginnings, who lived in an HDB apartment in Singapore with her mother, with only $5000 in her bank account, had just inherited a multi-million-dollar hotel empire. I was sure I would wake up, at any moment, soaked in sweat and realize that all of this was just a dream.

I was stood there in a beautiful room, courtesy of Mr Chan, at my very own wedding, planned by my best friend's sister, wearing a pearl-white, wedding dress, a sparkly diamond tiara in my hair. I was, by any definition, a blushing bride.

As I was led out of the room and down the stairs to the lobby by Loretta, I felt a bit like a Hollywood star.

'Keep calm. Just breathe,' she muttered to me as we walked. As we reached the ground floor, we turned a corner and I caught a glimpse of myself in a huge, antique mirror. I felt a wave of emotion flood over me. Of course, I knew what I looked like. I had just spent the past hour staring at myself in the suite upstairs, for goodness' sake, but still, catching myself unawares like that, I couldn't quite believe that I was that young woman in the wedding dress. Yes, that was *me*.

I was about to walk up an aisle of flowers to the new Terrace Room within the newly branded Duxton Heritage Reserve Hotel, with one hundred people watching my every move. Oh, God!

Oh, God! What was I thinking? As I saw the heavy double doors of the Terrace Room ahead of me, I started to panic and my fingers tightened around my bouquet. This was never going to work. I must have been mad. Why was I doing this? I couldn't do it. I needed to run away. But there was nowhere to run and Loretta had me in a firm armlock. There was no alternative but to carry on walking forward and look confident.

The two bridesmaids, the nieces of a family friend were waiting with posies in their hands at the door. Sally had offered to be their guardian and make sure they were ushered like little lambs in the right direction. The people around me smiled and sighed over my dress. The wedding planner, Loretta's sister, Zee, snapped her fingers and a string orchestra started up.

'Clara!' I looked up. It was Ken in a white, linen suit. 'You look amazing.' He beamed at me.

'Really?'

'Yes. Spectacular!' he asserted, firmly. He stepped forward, adjusted my tiara and then stood back to appreciate his handiwork. 'There. Perfect.'

'Ready?' prompted Loretta.

'I guess so,' I said. I could feel the contents of my stomach trying to escape. Then I channelled my thoughts to memories of Pauline and her beatific smile. It had always been radiant and warm. I could picture her right now, standing beside me, along with my mother, holding my hand. I felt myself begin to relax and calm down. It was working. I felt better.

'I'm here dear.' As if on cue, my mother appeared looking wonderful in a light blue suit. Her face was beaming a broad smile. Now, everything was perfect.

The double doors swung open, and I heard the rustle of one hundred people simultaneously turning in their seats. The string orchestra changed its music score and started to play something very beautiful. I had no idea what it was, but it sounded perfect. It calmed me somehow and the bridesmaids began to follow me up the aisle, with Sally walking behind them.

I felt euphoric. I was walking into an enchanted forest of people and flowers, carried on the swell of music. Fairy lights twinkled overhead. Beautiful flower arrangements were giving off their fragrance as I edged forwards, step by step. I swear I could almost hear birds chirruping above me. Flowers magically bloomed with each of my steps and people gasped as they looked up at me and followed me with their eyes. My uncle, Chin Wei's face caught my eye, beaming. It was the first time I had seen him dressed in a suit.

And there was Nicholas up ahead, my handsome prince charming, stood with his hands crossed in front of him, waiting for me. Mike and John at his side.

I started to fully relax and savoured every moment. I wanted to take it all in and remember it forever. The music played on. With jewels in my hair and the most beautiful dress I had ever worn. A different dress I add to the one I wore in London. A fresh dress for a new start in life. I knew I would never again experience anything like this. Ever. At least I hoped not.

Everything was perfect. No negative thoughts would be allowed into my head. As I reached the top of the aisle, I slowed my pace, breathing in the atmosphere, taking in the flowers and their amazing perfume, trying to impress every little detail into my mind, savouring every magical second.

I reached Nicholas and handed my bouquet to Loretta. I smiled warmly at John and Mike—then took Nicholas by the hand. He gave my fingers a gentle squeeze and I squeezed back. The registrar stepped forward, in a dark, vaguely clerical-looking outfit. She gave me a tiny, conspiratorial smile before addressing the congregation.

'Hello, everyone. Good afternoon. We are gathered here together to witness the love between two people. We are here to watch them pledge their love for each other. And to join with them in celebrating the joy of their new lives together. God blesses all who love, and God will certainly bless Clara and Nicholas today as they exchange their wedding vows.'

She took a breath, 'Do you, Clara Tan, love Nicholas Tate? Do you pledge yourself to him for better and for worse, for richer and for poorer, in sickness and in health? Do you put your trust in him now and forever?' She paused for my response.

My entire life flashed before me like a speeding bullet train. I was poised to hear someone shout out an objection. I could hear murmurs swelling from the congregation in anticipation of my turning tail and making a run for it. I felt my hand being squeezed again.

'Yes. Yes, I do,' I said, unable to withhold the tiny tremor in my voice. One hundred people released a breath.

'Do you, Nicholas Tate, love Clara Tan? Do you pledge yourself to her for better and for worse, for richer and for poorer, in sickness and in health? Do you put your trust in her now and forever?'

'An absolute yes,' declared Nicholas firmly, 'I do.' He beamed at me.

'May the both of you be blessed and may you have happiness always,' the registrar said warmly and looked challengingly around the room as though daring anyone to contradict her. My fingers tightened convulsively around Nicholas's. 'Now, come everyone let us applaud the happy couple.' Her part of the ceremony complete, she smiled at both of us, just as relieved as we were. 'You may kiss your bride,' she concluded with aplomb.

As Nicholas leaned in to kiss me, the chatter and applause broke out. We held what seemed to be a long kiss. My first kiss from my husband. Oh, God, I was married. I could see Maureen out of the corner of my eye, surreptitiously wiping her eyes. I looked for my own mother and espied her. Loretta had her arm around her. She looked radiantly happy.

Nicholas's father, Jack, stepped forward and whispered something in Nicholas's ear. Nicholas then turned to me, looking like a naughty boy who had stolen the cakes. Very guilty.

'What about the ring? I forgot the ring,' said Nicholas.

I thought for a moment, wondering what to do. Nicholas then turned to both Mike and John, to ask them for the ring. John then started to look guilty.

'No, forget it, darling. It's okay,' I said, still smiling, although my heartbeat had accelerated so much that I could barely breathe. I kept waiting for someone to stand up and say, 'It's okay, no big deal . . .' But no one did. No one said anything. I could only hear whispers.

Until. I met the eye of the even guiltier looking registrar—then quickly looked away before anyone noticed and heaped blame on her. But wasn't it her job to remember these things?

Loretta stepped forward and took my hand firmly, tugging me towards Nicholas. I could see that Nicholas was wondering what Loretta was doing.

'Come on. Hand me the ring!' she demanded. John fumbled in the pocket of his waistcoat, drew out the ring and handed it to Loretta. Nicholas was still looking like a deer caught in the beam of headlights at this point. Loretta then handed the ring to Nicholas, who promptly then placed the ring on my finger without further ado. 'There. All done. All happy now?'

'Thank you,' I whispered.

Loretta smiled, clasping my bouquet to her chest. 'That's all I've ever wanted. Just you to be happy.'

Before I could reply, 'Excuse me,' said the photographer, 'if I could get just the two of you. The bride and groom . . .'

Loretta returned my bouquet and ducked away. I adopted my most radiant, newlywed expression. Then, one by one, followed by small groups of people, the wedding guests came forward to take photographs with us. I smiled happily.

'Hang on,' Nicholas said, 'did she pronounce us husband and wife? And don't we have to sign something?' he sounded worried. There was a blinding flash and we both blinked.

Loretta had overheard Nicholas. 'Excuse me,' she said to the registrar, 'are they married? Did you pronounce them husband and wife?'

'That's a good shot!' said the photographer. 'Stay like that.'

'Oh, shut up, man,' Maureen pushed him aside. 'Well, are they?' Maureen's eyes were ablaze. She looked more like a grizzly bear than ever.

Nicholas tried to calm her down. 'Mum. It's okay. No big deal.'

'Not now, my boy. I'm just getting warmed up.' With that, Jack, John and Mike ranged beside her is a show of family solidarity.

'Well . . .' the registrar began softly.

'Well . . . are they married or are they not?' Maureen bridled. The room had fallen silent—all eyes on the registrar.

'I now pronounce you man and wife,' saying which, the registrar signed the marriage certificate, handed it shakily to Maureen and then fled.

'I suggest that we all go and get pissed now,' said Maureen.

'Hear, hear!' Jack agreed. Not wishing to defy Maureen, everyone just followed her out like sheep.

The string orchestra struck up the 'Bridal March' and a team of hotel staff ushered the guests towards the ballroom where the banquet would be served.

Nicholas looped his arm through mine and we walked down the aisle and out through the main doors.

'Silly woman,' Nicholas laughed. 'A whole bloody forest of flowers, a hundred people, a big white dress and we were almost not married.' I could see the funny side, too.

We reached the back of the room for a final session of photographs.

'Call me crazy—but this is fun,' he said, still laughing.

'Yes, it is. This is our wedding, and everything is okay now,' I kissed him for the cameras.

We went into the ballroom. A few hours later, we had feasted on an amazing four-course dinner with seafood, roast beef, roast pork and even caviar. We had drunk toasts. It had all gone according to plan. We cut the wedding cake with a huge silver knife, and everybody cheered.

The band started to play 'The Way You Look Tonight' and Nicholas led me on to the dance floor. That was one of those moments that I would keep in my scrapbook forever. A whirl of white and gold and glitter and music, Nicholas's arms around me, my head giddy from champagne and the knowledge that this was it, this was the high and soon it would be over.

The party was in full swing. The band was playing, and the dance floor was full. Amid the throng of beautifully dressed family, friends and strangers, I could pick out familiar faces: Loretta, dancing with her new date, a man whom she had chatted up in the church I think, and Ken deep in conversation with one of the waiters.

There was Jack, dancing very energetically with Maureen. There was a glow in her cheek and she looked about as animated as I had ever seen her. Glittering with an impressive array of diamonds, she was in a sweeping, pale-green evening dress and looked like the belle of the ball, which, in a way, she was. She had paid for everything and not once had she made a big deal of it.

It was wonderful to see everyone so happy. It was great to be a guest at your own event and that was kind of what I felt I was.

A group of women passed by, chattering and I heard snatches of their conversation.

'Spectacular . . .'

'So imaginative . . .'

They smiled at me and I smiled back. My face felt a bit stiff after having smiled all day long.

'Great party, Clara,' Ken said. 'Great band. Christ, I'd forgotten how much I love to dance.' I surveyed his appearance in dismay.

'Ken,' I said worriedly, 'you have split the rear of your trousers.'

'I know. They were too tight,' he shrugged, coolly.

Zee came over, 'Now, Clara,' she lowered her voice, 'do you want to wrap things up soon or keep going?'

'Oh, already?' I look instinctively at my wrist, but I wasn't wearing a watch. Not even my rubber band.

'The car's waiting outside,' said Zee. 'The driver has all the details. He'll take you to Changi VIP terminal and show you where to go. It's a different procedure for private planes, but it should be fairly straightforward. Any problems, you call me.' She lowered her voice to a whisper, 'You should be in Bali in a few hours. I really hope it all works out.'

I hugged her tightly. 'Zee . . . you're a star,' I muttered, 'I don't know what to say.'

'Clara, believe me, this is nothing. That young man would give you ten planes if you wanted them.' She hugged me back and then glanced at her watch. 'You had better find Nicholas. I'll see you in a bit.'

'Clara,' said Ken, 'did I just catch the words "private plane"?'

'Er . . . yes. Yes, you did.'

'You're flying on a private plane?'

'Yes.' I tried to sound nonchalant. 'We are. It's Maureen and Jack's wedding present to us.'

Ken shook his head. 'Damn. You know, I was planning to get you that myself. It was between that and a new toaster . . .'

'Idiot!' I laughed and then went off in search of my husband.

I found Nicholas cornered by two corporate types who apparently needed some marketing help. He leapt up gratefully as soon as I appeared. We went around the crowded room, saying our good-byes and thanks to all the guests. To be honest, it didn't take that long.

Finally, we approached the top table and interrupted Maureen as discreetly as we could.

'Mum, we're going now,' said Nicholas.

'Now?' Maureen frowned. 'It's too early.'

'Well . . . we're going, Mum. Where's Dad?'

'Thank you for a wonderful wedding,' I said, hugging her. 'It was really amazing. Everyone's been saying how wonderful it was.' I kissed her. 'Good-bye.'

'Not good-bye, Clara, babes,' she said firmly, 'not good-bye, my boy.'

'Good-bye, Mum,' said Nicholas, just as firmly. Their eyes met in a silent clash of wills. But then, she just leaned forward and kissed Nicholas on the cheek.

'Clara!' Someone nudged my shoulder. 'Clara, you're not going yet!' I turn around to see Zee looking flustered.

'Er . . . yes. We're off. Thank you so much for everything you've—'

'You can't go yet!'

'No one'll notice,' I said, glancing around the party.

'They have to notice! We have an exit planned, remember? The rose petals? The music?'

'Forget the exit?'

Zee stared, 'Are you joking? Orchestra!' she said urgently into her headpiece. 'Segue to "Some Day". Do you copy? Segue to "Some Day".'

She raised the walkie-talkie, 'Lighting crew, stand by with rose petals.'

'Zee,' I said helplessly. 'Honestly, we just wanted to slip away quietly—'

'My brides do not slip away quietly! Cue fanfare,' she muttered into her headpiece. 'Lighting crew, prepare exit spotlight.'

The thunderous fanfare of trumpets startled the guests on the dance floor, making them jump out of their skins. The lighting changed from the disco effect to an incandescent pink glow and the band started to play 'Some Day My Prince Will Come'.

'Go, you two,' said Zee, giving me a little shove. 'Go! *One* two three, *one* two three . . .'

'I told you, my little chickens, that you were not leaving yet,' Maureen laughed triumphantly.

Exchanging looks, Nicholas and I make it on to the dance floor, where the guests parted like the Red Sea to let us through. The music surrounded us, a spotlight followed our path, and suddenly, rose petals rained down gently from the ceiling.

This was rather lovely. I could hear 'aahs' and 'oohs' as we went by. The glow of the pink light was like being inside a rainbow, and the rose petals smelled wonderful as they drifted down on us. Nicholas and I were smiling at each other, and there was a petal in his hair—

'Stop!'

I felt a sudden chill, right down to the marrow of my bones.

The double doors had been flung open, and there he was, framed in the doorway, dressed in a black suit. The orchestra petered out uncertainly.

'Jared?' exclaimed Nicholas in astonishment. 'What are you doing here?'

'Having a good wedding, Nicholas?' he jeered.

'Come in,' I interrupted. 'Come on in and join the party. We would have invited you . . .'

'I know what you're doing, Clara.'

'We are now married,' I said blithely. 'No prizes for guessing that!'

'I know exactly what you have done,' snarled Jared. 'I object.'

'I think you're a bit late, my dear. Now piss off while you still can,' Maureen was truculent.

'And who are you to tell me anything, you old bag?' Jared sneered.

'Now, hang on. That's my mother,' Nicholas was now angry.

'I think everyone here needs to know that I love Clara and you stole her from me.'

'What are you doing, Jared. Are you drunk?' Nicholas demanded.

'Drunk or not, I'll knock his teeth out. No one speaks to my woman like that,' Jack rolled up his sleeves pugnaciously.

'Easy, Dad. Not worth it; not today of all days,' Mike cut in.

'Code red! Code red!' I heard Zee's voice crackling from the bouquet. 'Urgent. Code red. Call security.'

'I just want what is mine,' said Jared.

'Stop. Everyone. Just stop!! This is my wedding day,' I turned to Maureen. 'I'm sorry Maureen that this man insulted you. He has clearly lost his mind. Jack, hang on for just one second.' I looked up at Nicholas. 'This is the man I love. This is the man I have married. One date with you, Jared, hardly constitutes love.'

I was running on pure adrenaline as I mustered all my kick-boxing skills, squared up to Jared, clenched my fist, drew back my arm and planted one on his jaw. He went down like a sack of coal and didn't move.

'That's for insulting my mother-in law.'

Even Maureen seemed taken aback. 'Now that's my girl,' she said grinning. Even Nicholas seemed proud. My heart was thumping so hard, I wasn't sure I could remain standing and my shoes hurt my feet. I reached for Nicholas's hand and he squeezed my hand. I just wanted to go now and get away.

I could hear people murmuring things like 'Did you see that?' and 'She kicked his ass!' A woman head-to-toe in Prada looked worshippingly at me like I was some superhero.

Zee broke the moment. 'Time for the rose petals and if they don't fall, I have a backup set.'

'Emergency rose petals?' I exclaimed in disbelief.

'Sweetheart, I have every eventuality covered,' she twinkled at me. 'This is why you hire a wedding planner!'

'I think you're worth every penny,' I put an arm around her and gave her a kiss.

'I think after all this drama, we both need to rest and unwind. We can fly out in the morning,' said Nicholas in my ear.

'Good idea.'

The music swelled once more and we started walking again as more rose petals cascaded from the ceiling. The wedding planners were amazing. People were crowding around us and applauding— was it just my imagination or were there tears of joy? At the end of the line, I saw Loretta leaning forward. I tossed my bouquet into her outstretched hands.

The heavy double doors swung shut behind us and we were finally out and alone at last in the silence of the plush corridor; empty but for the two cleaning staff.

'We did it,' I said, laughing half in relief, half in exhilaration. 'Nicholas, we did it!'

Epilogue

'Oh shit!' The first words out of my mouth this morning was far from ladylike, but we had to checkout and we also had a flight to catch and a honeymoon to enjoy, and we were already running late. A sun-drenched, private villa on the island of Bali awaited our arrival. I looked at my phone to check the time.

'Shit.' I really must stop saying that, but it was 8.30 a.m. already and I hadn't even packed my bag yet. I looked over at Nicholas and noticed that he was beginning to stir.

'Breakfast, we need breakfast,' I whispered in his ear.

'Don't worry we have plenty of time,' he responded sleepily, at which point I reminded him that we didn't. I knew this because I needed exactly thirty minutes to get showered and packed. Not to mention the time to say goodbye to Loretta and Ken and get to the airport.

The next hour or so went by in a complete blur. I remembered walking past the ballroom on our way to the main entrance of the hotel and hugging both Loretta and Ken on the way out. I recalled telling them that they were in charge and instructing them to not burn the hotel down while I was away.

Within a few hours, we had arrived in Bali. Heaven with sand. Having settled in, we started to relax and enjoy our surroundings.

At this moment, having slept the first night like a baby, I was lying in the biggest and most comfortable bed in the world, in one of the most beautiful villas in a tropical paradise, feeling all dreamy and contented and happy, letting the rays of the morning sunlight dance on my closed eyelids. I stretched my arms above my head, reclining in an enormous mound of marshmallow-like pillows. Oh, I felt good. I felt . . . satiated. The previous night had been passionate. It was absolutely . . . well, let's just say it was awesome in every respect.

I sat up and reached for my cup of freshly ground and brewed coffee. Nicholas had made it for me just before he went off for a swim in the beautiful pool right outside our bedroom. He was now in the shower, so it was just me, alone with my thoughts.

It wasn't just Nicholas—although the whole thing was . . . well, beyond amazing. God, he really knew how to please a girl . . . Anyway. The point was, it wasn't just Nicholas and it wasn't about the morning coffee. It wasn't even about the villa and the fact that we were on vacation again. The fourth time in six months, but hey, who was counting?

Research. I called it research into other hospitality establishments. I discovered nuggets of information that I used to make the Duxton Heritage even better. In fact, the hotel was doing well. So well that we were booked solid for the next twelve months and I promoted Loretta to GM. She was amazing at it. And before you wonder why Loretta and not Ken, it's because women need career breaks and deserve to be given a chance. Just as I had been given one by Mr Chan. Besides, Ken had no interest in management—he told me as much.

I hadn't had an anxiety attack in months. When I looked back at the past year and how I used to be—well, it made me want to laugh really. This new Clara was so much more level-headed, calm and balanced. So much more responsible and confident. It was as though the tinted glasses I must have had on had fallen off— and suddenly I could see what was important in the world and what wasn't.

I had also been thinking that morning that I might open a hotel in Bali. A boutique hotel for couples who wanted to rediscover life. Nicholas and I had discussed it a little the previous night over dinner and I must say, I came up with a lot of interesting ideas. 'I think I was getting to be almost as good at marketing as Nicholas himself now, even if I say so myself.'

Perhaps I was crazy, but I had the financial means now, so why not? I had Mr Chan to thank for that. He had changed my life.

I casually reached for the remote control and switched on the television, planning to watch the news. I surfed the channels, trying to find *CNBC* or *Channel News Asia*, but the TV seemed stuck on the rubbish cable channels. Eventually I gave up, left it on something about the history of the Vikings or something and leaned back into my pillows.

The truth, I thought, taking a sip of the coffee, was that through all the changes in my life, from being a humble Client relationship manager, meeting the man of my dreams, and inheriting a hotel chain, I was still the same old Clara. I hadn't changed at all really. I was still of course a little bit anxious, but that was part of me too. That was probably why Nicholas and I got on so well.

Nicholas. Yes, that was a nice thought. I wondered where he was. His shower was taking a long time. I sat up in bed and was just considering going into the bathroom to surprise him when he appeared in the doorway. He had a white towel wrapped round his waist and droplets of water glistened on his shoulders.

'I'm just popping out for a little fresh air. D'you want to come?' he asked.

'No, you go ahead. I'm just going to enjoy this bed for a little while longer. Then I will get up, I promise.'

'Okay. See you shortly, then.'

I reached for the remote and zapped the TV to a different channel. A nature program. Yes, that was more like it. There was a close up of a tiny lion cub and a sombre voice-over talking about the effects of drought on the ecosystem. I turned up the volume and settled back, pleased with myself. I was going to learn about this lion cub and the ecosystem and global warming. Perhaps Nicholas and I could talk about all these important issues over breakfast.

This day was turning out to be perfect. And it was only nine a.m.!

I turned off the nature program, snuggled back down under the covers and closed my eyes for a few moments. Maybe Nicholas and I would spend all day here, in this lovely room. Maybe we would have oysters and champagne sent over.

Nine o'clock, interrupted a little voice in my head. I frowned for a second and shook my head to get rid of it. But it continued to niggle annoyingly at the back of my mind. Nine o'clock. Nine . . .

I sat up bolt upright, my eyes wide in dismay. Oh, my God!

Nine thirty. Nicholas.

I had booked a private boat charter to one of the islands, inclusive of lunch. *I had promised him we would do something nice today.* And here I was, with half an hour to go, still lolling in bed. I had to get ready. Oh, God.

I switched off the TV, buried my head in my hands and tried to think calmly and rationally. Okay, if I got going straight away, we could make it. If I got dressed as quickly as possible, ran downstairs and we jumped in a taxi—we just might make it. The harbour, from where the boat would leave was just down the road. We had a grace time of quarter of an hour for lateness, hadn't we? We could still do the trip. It could still happen. In theory. We were on vacation anyway and it was a private charter, so why was I rushing. Nicholas could go for a coffee while I got ready.

'Hi,' said Nicholas, popping his head around the bedroom door.

'Nicholas. Is everything okay?' I asked.

'Yup. I somehow knew you would be late, so I changed our boat schedule to be a couple of hours later. I've been waiting for you to surface,' he grinned.

'Thank you. That was thoughtful!'

'Oh, and guess what? I had the most wonderful . . .' And then broke off, I wasn't sure why. 'Come on . . . let's go grab some breakfast.'

'Okay,' I clambered out of bed.

As we strolled down to the local beach restaurant for breakfast, I couldn't not ask.

'You said you had something to show me,' I prompted.

'Yes, I did. But you will have to wait and see.' I squinted in puzzlement. After our breakfast of tropical fruit and delicate pastries, we set off to the harbour. The yacht looked amazing and the crew welcomed us aboard.

It took me barely five seconds to realize what was going on. Not two yards from me were Ken and Loretta.

'Oh, my God. How did you guys get here?' A dumb question because they had obviously flown in on a plane just as we had done.

'Your darling husband invited us over for the weekend,' said Loretta, hugging me.

'And I wasn't going to say no,' laughed Ken, joining us in the hug.

'I figured all you guys needed a break, so I hope that was okay,' said Nicholas. Ken and Loretta beamed. My week had just been made, as if this vacation couldn't get any better.

As we set sail into the sun, the wind in our hair, I felt a tingle of pleasure as Nicholas came up from behind me and nuzzled my ear.

'Hi, beautiful, I hope you liked the surprise.'

'It was wonderful and so thoughtful.'

Life was going to be amazing with this man, and I was sure we would have many, many more adventures to come. Don't worry, I promise to tell you all about them. Best of all, I'm going to start my diary again. An entire new adventure to document.

The Duxton Heritage Reserve

'The best heritage hotel in Singapore' read the blurb on the front-page announcement of the *Straits Times*. It seemed that the old dame, formally the Duxton Hotel, had survived and was even better than before. Another decade of existence was assured, thanks to the innovations of Clara and Nicholas.

The Duxton had risen, like the mythical phoenix from the ashes of its former self and was on its way to scale new heights. Its walls still whispered secrets of its illicit past: a spice-trading hub at one time; an illegal distillery at another. But now, new blood coursed through its mortar veins and the thirty-seven renovated rooms offered its guests a majestic vintage and modern décor which evoked a timeless feel. The two restaurants promised to seduce your taste buds with its fusion cuisine from around the world, or the simple comforts of local favourites. However long you stayed within its walls, you would leave feeling refreshed, joyful and determined to return.

The old Duxton had gone to sleep, but the new beginning had ushered in a new era with a new jewel that sparkled timelessly in the middle of Singapore.

Pay it a visit sometime and see it for yourselves. You may just run into Clara or Nicholas. But to do so, you will have to get past Ken and Loretta first.

Acknowledgements

My love for writing will live forever. I, however, will not. But it is my hope that my work will remain long after I am done, even if only in which to wrap fish.

Writing this book was tremendous fun; researching it even more so. I love humour and look for it every day. It can enrich our lives and bring balance. So, to those who kept me smiling, I want to say thank you. To all my close friends, you know who you are, and need not be named one by one, I thank you. To the friends of friends who offered to read early drafts, I say thank you as well. To my fearless editors and to my awesome publishers at Penguin Random House, I offer my gratitude, thanks and respect to you all.